SHADOW OF THE VULTURE

REGINA GARZA MITCHELL

T0155147

DEATH'S HEAD PRESS

an imprint of Dead Sky Publishing, LLC
Miami Beach, Florida
www.deadskypublishing.com

Cover Art: Justin T. Coons

The "Splatter Western" logo designed
by K. Trap Jones

Book Layout: Lori Michelle
www.TheAuthorsAlley.com

Para mi familia.

1

THEY HAD BEEN fighting for months, the battles moving as each side pushed forward and fell back. This was to be the last battle. They had lost too many men and the other side hadn't lost enough. Cannons were delivered and wheeled out on the field. Some of the men were afraid of the iron weapons, scared they would blow themselves up. And they probably would. Juana and Analisa took charge of one, working together to load the heavy iron balls and fire them. They had wounded several and killed a few men, each splash of red energizing them. For the first time, they felt they could win this fight. They had to, or the invaders would continue creeping in, taking over. Ravages and plundering had happened in Mexico already. Juana was determined it wouldn't happen to her parents, to her home.

She finished tamping down the barrel and turned to her friend. Analisa's usual smile was on her face, and then the left side of her head disappeared in a squelch of red-black. Smoke rose from her seared skin. She remained standing for a moment before crumpling to the ground. The world shifted, and

Juana felt herself fall. Knew she would continue falling for the rest of her life. But she was still on her feet and there was no time to help, no time to mourn or comprehend what had just happened. She had to fire the weapon herself.

It didn't matter who had done it. *They* were all responsible. Taking the land and now the one person she loved most. The person who had trusted her and followed her here. *She thought you would watch over her, be her guardian angel*, Juana thought. *But you let her die. Let them kill her. Analisa is dead.* The word echoed down the empty chamber that was her mind.

Juana fired the cannon, the heavy ball falling uselessly to the ground not hitting anyone. She looked around. Men were strewn on both sides of the field, some hurt, some dead. Some fell as she watched, bodies thudding quietly amidst the roar of cannon and rifle fire and screaming voices. Not all who fell were dead. She ran. Over the empty part of the field to the other side, ignoring the oft unreliable revolver in its holster on her hip, grabbing instead the knife her father had brought her from Monterrey. The shaft and hilt were pure silver, blessed by a curandero for protection. Symbols and sigils decorated its handle; she didn't know what the designs meant, but she knew they were powerful. *Should've given it to Analisa.* Her hat flew off her head and her hair blew around her face.

"A woman!" screamed an enemy soldier, a mix of rage and bemusement on his face. "Look at this crazy bitch! What the fu—"

Her knife cut off the man's next words, slurring

them into a gurgle as she slashed across his mouth, his jutting tongue, and down his throat, relishing the warmth of the stream as it flowed out of him.

She spit on him before moving on, conjuring up all of the hatred she could into the wad of phlegm. She yelled and cursed like a mad woman as she thrust and stabbed, feeling the suck of flesh, the jolt of bone. She didn't care anymore, looked forward to joining Analisa. But she would take some of these bastards with her, would continue fighting them all the way to hell. The knife grew slippery, but she held it tightly, thrusting, pulling, stabbing, slashing. The blade was sharp and did its work well, as though enjoying its purpose. She was joined by others with swords and knives, taking this gun-reliant army by surprise. They didn't know the meaning of true courage, the rush of closing in on your enemy, feeling his guts with your fingers, squeezing the slippery entrails to make him scream, the insertion of blade through skin that parted as easily as a whore's thighs. The sheer delight of bathing in the blood of your enemies, knowing they would breathe no more because of you. Juana laughed in someone else's voice as she wielded her knife, a loud keening that sounded more like crying.

Only she never cried.

Eventually it ended, one side or both retreating. Juana's arm was numb, her torn clothes covered in bits of flesh and gore, flies landing and relanding.

I am clothed in the body of my enemies.

She wanted to laugh. Felt the flies' spindly legs like tongues lapping the blood off her skin. Her right hand was stuck in a fist, curled tightly around the knife; she could not open her hand. It wouldn't respond. The flies continued to buzz and scratch and taste. A cloud of gnats and flies hovered around her, landing and tasting the grue on her skin, her clothes. One crawled over her lips as she licked them, feeling its spindly legs before it lazily flew up and landed on her cheek. Her arm felt weighted down. She could barely move, could only look around her.

The bodies on the field hummed with insects taking sustenance from the fallen. She wondered how long it would take before they laid eggs inside of the fallen bodies. Crows had begun to peck choice bits from the bodies of the fallen, stretching meat and muscle until it tore free so they could swallow it down.

The velvet touch of fly legs on her face sent her over the edge as they fed off the flecks of flesh and blood coating her skin. She vomited, her right fist still curled around the knife so tightly the sigils imprinted themselves as on her palm. The pool of sick drew some of the flies away, its rancid odor an invitation to yet another feast. But the meatier scent of her grue-covered skin retained its allure for some. She shooed them away with her left hand while her aching right arm dangled. She stepped back, not wanting to see the damaged bodies around her, only wanting Analisa. But not the way she was now. She didn't dare think the word, but death was all around. She wore it in the streaks of red-brown on her clothing, her skin. Tasted and smelled its putrescence. Death was everywhere on the battlefield. It was the living who intruded.

She plodded back across the field, stepping over downed men until she reached the cannon. Analisa lay there, her remaining eye looking surprised, half of her face stuck in a smile.

"Pretty bad, yeah?" Analisa said. She stood beside Juana, also looking down at her dead body. "At least it was quick. And I didn't piss myself like Roberto did." She shook her head. "That poor guy. What a way to go."

"But . . . "

"I know. It's weird."

Juana shook her head, closed her eyes. Opened them.

Analisa still stood there beside her, still lay on the ground. A line of small, red ants had begun a trail into the good side of her mouth. Black insects covered her eyes and drank from the blood that spilled out of her body.

Juana looked again at her ruined friend standing beside her and gave in to the darkness.

2.

JUANA SAT IN the scrub eating a piece of salted meat, watching a kettle of vultures soar eastward, wondering if they would find Pepe where she left him on the side of the road. She would have buried him, but it was too hot, and she had too far to go to waste time burying a burro. Even if he had been her last living friend. She'd named him after her youngest brother who'd died when he was five. They had the same dumb, sad brown eyes that looked at her with a pleading she didn't understand. Just as with the original Pepe, she'd done what she could to take care of him, to make him comfortable. This Pepe had been with her since the war ended. She had lost track of time, but it felt like ages. The war was over and a large chunk of Mexico now belonged to the United States. It made her blood boil to think of it. Skirmishes still broke out. The Anglos in particular didn't think much of their neighbors, the people they killed and stole from and molested. Their destiny, their god, told them the land was theirs. Their god apparently never told them they didn't have to steal it; there was room for all if they hadn't been greedy.

If they hadn't needed to control everything. If they hadn't made the mistake of thinking other people were savages when they were the ones engaging in savagery. But here they were. And here she was, wandering from place to place, trying to figure out where she belonged, what to do next. She had thought of being a vaquera, but those days were at an end with most of the ranches split apart or gone completely. It was a new world.

She wandered the new world and made do as a bounty hunter, bringing in the occasional bounty. She hunted the real criminals, the ones who killed people because of their skin color or nationality, on her own, leaving their bodies to be found or not. She fought her own war with her own code of ethics.

For now, though, she wandered, sticking to la frontera. She laughed to think of the fictitious border conjured up by the lying Anglos. This country, that country. The land belonged to itself, and the only borders were the ones created by men. But the Anglos weren't content with stealing the land. Now they were taking ranches and farms from the people whose families had been settled in the area for hundreds of years. But only those of Spanish and Mexican descent. A new war had begun, one without a name.

She rolled her sleeves up, brushing away the inevitable dust that stuck to her arms, and stretched before sipping from a flask of water. Analisa stood by a mesquite tree a few yards away.

"Where will you go now?" she asked. "Do you think you can kill them all on your own?" She smiled her strange half-smile. The other half was gone, crushed into a gleaming red-black hole in her face.

7

Her left eye was mashed to a pulp, the slimy socket gaping where her face had been blown apart. Juana was used to her now, the way she had looked since that bastard killed her.

It had always been the two of them, ever since she could remember. They grew up together, defying Juana's mother who was horrified at her daughter playing with a peone child, a servant's daughter. But they were inseparable. Analisa had been there when her brother Pepe died, the only one who saw Juana's tears, who knew she felt responsible. Juana was ten years old and loved the sickly child from the first time she saw him. They all did, even Juana's mother who tended to aloofness, as though she knew he wasn't long for the world and wanted to make up for it.

Juana was her disgrace: undignified, unladylike, and with no interest in becoming a lady. She took art lessons from the tutor her mother hired and learned to read and write Spanish, English, and French, which her mother later thought had been a mistake. Rather than becoming genteel, Juana snuck into her father's library and read books, mostly the adventure stories that were his favorites. Even worse, she bought books of her own, adventures about men who fought and killed and led unrefined lives. That was where she got her ideas and what eventually led to her decision to enlist and fight in the war. She had learned bravery from men in books, and it never occurred to her that women could not also be brave.

Everything Juana had for herself she wanted for Analisa. The two developed their own codes to leave notes for each other in the dirt, on the walls, or on small scraps of paper Juana accumulated. As they grew older, Analisa gravitated toward boys, and sometimes girls. She enjoyed people. Juana, on the other hand, grew more solitary. She had no desire to marry. She simply wanted to be left alone with her books, the sketches she occasionally made in the leatherbound journals her father bought for her, and her friend. But she also desired adventure, an itch that kept her constantly searching for something. Constantly in trouble. She couldn't sit still other than when she was reading; there was something more, something she was meant to do. She found her opportunity when the war started.

When she heard that men were refusing service to their country—some even joining the invader's ranks—Juana decided to offer her own services. She endured her mother's disapproval, the taunts and jibes from her older brothers and anyone else who found out her plan. Only her father believed her. Believed *in* her. He was the one who wrote the letter to General González detailing her seriousness and calling on their lineage, their status, her father's own past service record. His only stipulation was that she should not go alone, and he included Analisa in his request. He knew the two would look out for each other. And they had. Until that day.

She walked for days, following the river. She avoided the trade routes and saw few people. She was in no rush, not sure where she would go next. She needed to restock her supplies soon, so she'd head to San Antonio. She could pick up a bounty or two while she was there, hear the latest news, and figure out what to do next. Aimless wandering suited her, but she was no longer satisfied. The scars on her palm had begun to itch lately as though trying to tell her something. Usually the feeling in her stomach let her know she was getting close to where she needed to be. The site of the next battle where she could wreak vengeance for Analisa.

"Or for yourself," Analisa whispered. Since she died, she had an annoying habit of knowing Juana's thoughts.

Juana shrugged her off. "Think what you want." Maybe the feeling in her stomach was just hunger.

She took on a few small jobs at ranches and farms in exchange for food, water, and some coin, restocking her water supply and washing herself. She had grown used to the smell of her own unwashed skin, the constant itch in her armpits, her breasts, and under the crop of hair that was growing back on her head, but it was always a relief to feel clean. Even if only for a little while. Some nights she stayed out in the open, camping near mesquite trees if she could. They reminded her of old women, guardians. She remembered a story Analisa told her once of how the trees held the spirits of dead women. They walked across the plains at night, gossiping and helping those in need. She did not see any trees walking, though, just coyotes and wild cats.

Analisa was her only company most of the time, her time in the towns reminding her of why she chose to be alone. She took on a few days' work at a small ranch called Las Nepantlas.

The work there was hard, keeping her too busy to think. At the end of her second day, she bathed in a stream away from the main house. A young woman walked by and saw her before she could cover up.

"It's you!" she said. "I've heard about the Angel of the Battlefield."

"Angel—really?" Analisa said, standing behind the young woman, shaking with laughter, the never-ending blood dripping out patterns on the ground as she clutched her stomach and hooted.

Juana tried to cover herself, angry at being found this way. "Angel of Death, maybe," Juana replied and let out a rusty laugh that sounded more like a croak as she tried to make sense of the patterns formed by Analisa's blood. How could she keep bleeding for so long? It had been weeks.

The woman looked at her and backed away, eyes wide.

"Thank you," Juana said, remembering that the woman could not hear Analisa. "I didn't mean . . . "

"I just wanted to pay my respects. I was told about the women who brought water to the men and tended to their needs, the nurses—"

Juana didn't hold back her anger. "That wasn't us! The men's wives or girlfriends did that. The women who believe men cannot care for themselves. We were all grateful." Her eyes flashed. "But that was not *us*. Was not me. We—I—fight!" She took a breath to stop herself from saying anything else.

The young woman's smile grew wider. "Then you are even more of an angel than I thought."

That night Juana ate well, a stew of goat meat, beans, and chile the woman, Yanina, brought her. She wanted Juana to sleep indoors—in her own bed, even—but Juana politely declined, ignoring

Analisa's amusement at the woman's undisguised interest.

"Turning down a good lay?" Analisa said as Juana lay down to sleep under the stars.

"You were the one who enjoyed that, not me."

"Then do it for me. It's been so long." Analisa sighed. "And no one could want me looking like this. But you . . . I could watch. It would be so lovely."

Juana shook her head. "I'm fine." Analisa was in her head, feeling her loneliness, but she didn't press.

A lone vulture circled the sky the next day as Juana continued her journey, laden with tortillas, salt pork, and fresh water that Yanina had pressed upon her before she left. She would eat well, at least until she made it to San Antonio. Juana admired the vulture's grace, the lazy way it moved its wings to keep the air pushing it ever up and forward. Her mother had hated the birds, but they couldn't help what they were, what they ate, anymore than Juana could help the way she was. They had a job to do, just like everyone else.

Juana hated thinking about her mother. They hadn't agreed on much, but she had done her best to indulge her only daughter. She'd had such hopes for Juana, hopes that were quashed as soon as Juana was old enough to speak her mind. Juana didn't want marriage or a husband or society. She wanted adventure and exploration and to be left alone. She certainly had plenty of that now.

The irony wasn't lost on her, that she went to fight the battles that were supposed to save the land and strengthen her country. What those invading men did to her parents was unforgiveable. To her mother, especially. Juana closed her eyes, thinking of the vulture soaring in the sky, the peace it must feel. At least her parents were with Pepe now. Padre Trujillo had explained that some people were too special to live, such was the case with Juana's brother. But Juana thought his specialness should have made it so that he was the one who survived, not her. Analisa, not her. Her mother, not her. And yet she kept on going, killing other people's loved ones in a never-ending quest for vengeance. Vengeance she was tiring of.

So much anger. So much death. She was tired of both.

"I should have eaten their hearts," she said. "Should have eaten them the way our ancestors did." She wondered how it would taste to bite down on such a firm muscle, chewing through its toughness to get to the center.

"You mean *my* ancestors?" Analisa asked. "Your ancestors were too delicate for that sort of thing, and killed mine for being barbaric." She snickered.

"You know what I mean. I should have cut them open and torn out their insides, eaten their guts."

"They had no valor, so why would you want to eat their hearts—to weaken yourself?" Analisa's lopsided smile was irritating today.

"To humiliate them. Abase them. Those cowards couldn't handle a woman besting them, for a woman to eat their hearts would be the ultimate insult."

"What are you, some kind of warrior goddess? 'I eat their hearts while they're still alive and make them watch.'" She rolled her eye. "Please. You've never craved greatness before. Is this a sign that you truly loved your little Analisa?" She batted her eye.

"You know I did," Juana said. "I do."

"You'd be a terrible goddess," Analisa said.

"That's why I'm a warrior."

Analisa kept her lopsided smile but said nothing. They kept walking.

She walked toward San Antonio, the shadow created by the vulture flying high above. She knew it couldn't be the same one each time, but something told her that the bird was her guide to whatever happened next.

3.

THE MEN RODE toward Jovita Flores's property in the late afternoon, just as the sun was beginning its descent.

Her jacal was situated on a small rise, too low to be called a proper hill but high enough to be kept safe from floods, even during the rainy season. It was close enough to the river that she could fetch water easily and bathe when she needed to, even now when her feet swelled up like rotten fruit ready to burst and walking felt like stepping on knives that stabbed and jabbed her twisted feet. When she was young and could still stand straight, she had cultivated a small oasis of trees and plants that surrounded the house and provided it shade. Her own forest in the desert. Agave, herbs, pepper plants, and aloe grew in a plot near the tiny kitchen building behind the house. A patch with a few rows of corn, beans, and pumpkin lay farther out on the property. Sunflowers and nopal grew along the rickety stick and maguey fence that defined her property line. Jovita hadn't wanted a fence; she believed land could not be owned. Like bodies they were merely borrowed for a time. But J.

C. Cavazos had insisted and built it himself when he gifted the property to her. And who was she to turn away such generosity?

The house wasn't much to look at from the outside, appearing to be little more than a dilapidated shack. Weathered boards bleached of color from years in the unrelenting sun, topped with a thick thatch of dried palm leaves. The same thatching lay over wooden beams behind the house, providing some relief during the day. Hers was a typical hut surrounded by an atypical amount of trees. But she cultivated this land for over half a century, time enough to see the trees and her gardens grow.

When she had settled here all those years ago, there was no Soledad. Only the Cavazos Rancho. Jesús Cristóbal Cavazos had inherited the ranch from his grandfather, whose own father had bought 125,000 acres and established what he envisioned as his legacy. Twenty-five years ago, he parceled off the land and sold it, along with the livestock, and the seeds of Soledad were planted The ranch had been split into smaller ranches and farms, and Soledad was now a proper town less than ten miles away and getting closer every day, filling up with more and more people. The railroad would bring it even closer, but they hadn't begun building it yet. She would likely be gone before it got too close. For that she was grateful. She did not want to see the land spoiled by metal and machines and smoke and the people who would inevitably follow. The influx had already begun, and these men were an unwelcome part of it.

She was tired. Jovita knew her time would be at an end soon and she would have to atone for the choices she'd made over the years. But for now, she was here and would do what she could before that time arrived. She headed to the gate to meet the Anglos. These were not men she wished to invite into her house.

They stopped short when they saw the old woman waiting at the gate. She wore a large black hat and a ratty rebozo decorated with feathers and beads. She leaned heavily on her bastón and greeted them as though they were expected.

A wiry man in a dirty brown hat dismounted and stepped forward, tipping his hat back so he could see her better, but not taking it off. Avery Gifford. The other five men's faces had darkened to desert hues, as though the sand had become part of their skin, but his had merely chapped. Red streaks blended with the dirt and sweat on his face. Tiny blisters puckered up where his skin had burned in the sun. *He should have put some aloe on that*, she thought. But he was the kind who would relish the pain and think himself stronger for it rather than just stupid. The kind who assumed the weather would adjust to him rather than the other way around. His eyes were small and hard, nearly lost in his deep brows. He beckoned to one of the others.

She recognized the dark young man who came forward. Juan Carlos. His grandparents had been peones, servants at the Cavazos rancho. His mother too. His father was probably Cavazos himself. He treated the peones like his own property, and the boy's eyes had a similar look. Carlos, as he was called, would not look directly at Jovita.

She chuckled and said, "I hope you didn't think

you would be invited in." Her words were distorted by her lack of teeth and the spittle that flew from her mouth.

"What the hell was that?" Avery asked. "Don't even sound like Mek'skin. Or look it. She's a dirty one, ain't she?" He spit a glob of tobacco juice on the ground. She was the ugliest thing he'd ever seen, and something about her was familiar, too, reminding him of a dream he'd had the night before, wings and sharp claws like knives. That made him uncomfortable, a feeling he didn't cotton to. "Well, what'd she say, boy?"

Carlos told him. He took care to speak slowly so as not to draw attention to his accent. Avery didn't like it when Carlos's accent "got in the way." Carlos kept his eyes on the ground, trying not to look at Jovita. She laughed when she saw Avery's anger at her words, showing her remaining teeth proudly. She hunched forward over the bastón, hands with swollen rounded knuckles curled like claws around the wood, reminding Carlos of a bird on a perch. The feathers in her rebozo reinforced the image. He wiped sweat from his brow.

The horses stamped impatiently as Avery took the old woman's measure. The men astride them looked tired. Angry. They had not planned for this, wanting instead to surprise the old woman in her house and instill fear.

There were stories about Jovita Flores, stories that Avery had laughed at. She ate aborted fetuses and newborn babies, crunching their bones after midnight. She had skinned a man alive and run her fingernails over the exposed musculature, licking bits of his body from her fingers greedily as he screamed, supposedly just for beating his wife. She hexed cattle, making them eat their own tongues and choke on the blood that flowed from it or cursed them so their milk was spoiled, forcing families to smell the rancid sourness as they dumped pails and pails of ruined milk before eventually slaughtering the animals. She had cursed a pregnant woman so that her baby was born backwards and with two heads, splitting its mother apart as it emerged into the world before being sold to a traveling show. The townspeople loved to talk about her, even if none admitted to knowing or dealing with her. Most still went to her when they needed help. Bruja was the word they used. Avery got a kick out of the stories, but in the end she was just a woman.

"I'm the new sheriff in Soledad, ma'am, and I'm here to introduce myself. I keep law and order and don't hold with no nonsense." He put on his town voice. The voice he used when he wanted to impress people. "I'm told that you ain't got a deed for this land you're livin' on. And that's a problem." He waited for Carlos to translate, still playing lawman. In truth, he had killed Sheriff Brett a few weeks before moving to town.

Her laugh surprised him. "Is that all you could come up with? I thought you'd have more imagination, but you're just another ignorant pig."

Carlos cringed. He couldn't repeat her words. Why did she have to be like this? The vieja was going to get herself hurt or worse. He took a deep breath and translated her words for Avery.

His yelp of laughter surprised Carlos. "The old

broad's got gumption, I'll give her that." He looked at Jovita. "It's $250 if you want to keep living here. That's a bit above the gov'ment price, but we'll just call that a convenience tax since I had to come all the way out here to speak with you. You got a week." He got back on his horse and started riding away before Carlos finished his translation.

"You should be ashamed of yourself," Jovita said when he was finished. The sky seemed to darken, but it was just a kettle of vultures passing overhead.

Carlos's face flushed with anger as he kept his eyes down, refusing to look directly at her. How dare she talk to him like that. He was just doing his job! He opened his mouth to retort but closed it when her shadow moved, changed to reflect outspread wings. He turned his eyes back to his horse and climbed on thinking, *bruja*.

Her voice intruded in his head. *No*, it said, *najuala*.

When he dared to look back, Jovita was gone as though she had flown away.

4.

TROUBLE WAS ON the horizon, though the men didn't know it yet. It was in the far-off echo of hooves pounding the ground. A sound they didn't hear over the noise of their own horses and the cattle they urged to the north.

The trails had been calm so far, the plains clear. Not even the buffalo roamed freely anymore. Too many people killing too many things. They'd only been on the trail about a month, and it would be a lot longer before they reached St. Louis. There was a lot of land left to cross, some of it Indian territory, but the cattle themselves were more of a concern than the people they might meet. There had been no major trouble yet, aside from the first week.

They were eating breakfast their third day out when a calf screamed. A group of large vultures had surrounded it on the ground, and others took turns swooping down from the air and tearing at it with their beaks. The calf was streaked with blood, and the vultures didn't back down even after the mother charged them. One flew up in the air, landed on the little one's head, and plunged its beak into one of the calf's eyes. It tore out a chunk of the eye before being head-butted by one of the larger cows. A cloudy pinkish fluid pulsed out of the torn orb   as the calf's bleat turned into a scream. The bird flew up, surprised, and immediately back down again to try for the other eye. A second bird jumped on the calf's tail and began burrowing into the soft flesh beneath, ripping its anus open with a razor-sharp beak. The calf's bleats grew frantic, and it fell to the ground as the larger cows tried to protect it.

"Don't shoot!" Lupe warned. The noise would agitate the rest of the herd even more, and they'd wind up with a stampede. He grabbed his rope and began swinging it, trying to scare the birds away. Octavio and Ignacio did the same while the rest of the men worked at keeping the cattle calm.

Eventually they were able to shoo the birds off of the calf, which by this time emitted a bleat that sounded like a child's scream. But a line of vultures remained in the nearby trees, heads moving in unison as they watched. One seemed less interested in the calf than the men. It stared, unblinking, as though watching them.

"This is not right," Ignacio said and made the sign of the cross. He muttered a prayer to la Virgen de Guadalupe.

The calf lay on its side, its damaged eye weeping milky fluid, the other half-closed. It lifted its head and turned toward the men, blood still seeping from its hindquarters. Small tears had formed one large wound, and at least one of the birds had managed to tear a gash in its stomach. Its sides moved in time with its weak panting breath, and it laid its head back down. Octavio walked over and slit its throat with his knife.

It took a long time to calm the herd, and they still had to finish packing up before they could move on. The vultures stared from their perches in the trees and on the ground. Watching. They only made a few miles that day. It had been quiet since then.

But the day wasn't over yet.

They stopped for the evening. It was hot and the cattle were slow. Tired. Octavio used his bandana to wipe his face and neck. He was weary, having ridden drag for the latter part of the day. It was tiring to ride at the end of the drive, trying to keep the slowest animals moving with the rest of the herd. The heat hit you worse for some reason. Maybe it was sympathy for the beasts. Or maybe it was being away from home for so long. He wondered how Sarah was doing, whether he'd be back before their baby came, hoping that his sister was taking good care of her. He thought of Sarah often to remind himself why he did this work. It would give them enough money for the next year or even two, even if they had to move. And he trusted the men out here with him. Most of them had been part of Soledad's militia before they'd been ordered to disband, and told that a sheriff would be hired. Not one of them, of course. They all knew that meant a gringo.

And then this opportunity came up. Someone Ignacio knew that needed good men who could speak English. The job paid fifty American dollars a month, and they'd be home within six months. That was more money than Octavio could make on his own or working as a farmhand. With this money, he could buy some land and start his own ranch. A place where Sarah could raise the baby. She and his sister, Mariluz, would take care of the house. Eventually he could hire his own men to work for him. Not many; he didn't want a large ranch. Just a piece of land where he could raise his own cattle, a few crops, and take care of his family on his own terms. They'd belong to nobody.

He let his thoughts wander as he saw to his horse, ignoring the soreness in his limbs. He wasn't on first guard duty tonight and would be able to catch a few hours of sleep soon.

They finished setting up camp for the night, and Felix was cooking pan de campo over a small fire while a pot of frijoles borrachos warmed to the side. Pedro finished seeing to the horses and went to tell the rest of the men that dinner would be ready soon. He was the youngest, still in his teens, but on his way to becoming a good man.

The men were relaxed and joking as they shook the dust from their clothes. They thought about their families and the much needed money they'd make.

The sun had nearly set when the Rangers showed up.

Their claim was cattle rustling.

A man with a neatly clipped black mustache did the talking as he sat on his horse. "My name's Jack Wallace." He doffed his worn brown hat and alit from his horse. "We're with the Texas Rangers. One

Obediah Bridges claims that cattle he legally purchased," he paused to flash a piece of paper with writing and signatures on it, "from Adelberto Jiménez were stolen. We were provided a description of the cattle and the men who took them, and I'm afraid y'all meet that description." He pointed at the herd. "Those cows bear the brand, and y'all need to surrender yourselves immediately. If you choose not to surrender yourselves, well . . . " The laugh was low and mean, reflecting the flint in his eyes.

Luís walked toward him and said in English, "This is obviously a misunderstanding. We have the papers here." He reached in his vest pocket, but before he could pull out the documents a shot was fired. Red bloomed across the right side of his chest, and a chunk of his arm went flying. Luís fell, a look of surprise on his face. Dust flew as the cows stomped their feet.

Octavio immediately grabbed for his gun and saw that the others were doing the same.

"Now, now, boys." Wallace raised his hands as if to prove he had nothing to do with the shot. "My men are jumpy, and we wouldn't want anyone else to get hurt. We just need for you all to come with us and the cattle to be returned. If you put down your arms, we promise you safe escort. We can get this sorted. But if you want to play rough, well, we can do that too. In fact, some of my men might prefer that. It's up to you."

Octavio and Lupe exchanged a glance. This wasn't good, but maybe they could get out of it. The rest of them looked at each other and nodded. Made a show of dropping their guns. Octavio thought of the knife he had stashed in his boot. He knew the others had them also. Being on the trail required it.

"That's good, boys. Real good." Jack smiled. "I won't bother asking for your knives 'cause we know you wouldn't try anything foolish." His laugh grated on Octavio's nerves as he watched the blood pooling around Luís. His face paled to grey. He had been a good man, a good trailboss. Who would tell his family?

The men walked toward each other at Jack's instruction, the Rangers' guns still aimed at them. Octavio didn't see Joseph and hoped he had the sense to stay hidden.

"We've got a wagon just over yonder, and we'd be much obliged if you'd walk over to it. You'll ride the rest of the way with us, and some of my gentlemen will take care of the cattle."

This wasn't good, but what choice did they have? They promised safe passage. Maybe they meant it. Octavio thought of Sarah and wondered if he'd ever get to see his child. He saw similar concern and anger in the others' faces. They all had people to get back to, homes and families. Lives. They'd do what they had to in order to get through this.

They were walking up the hill when the Rangers opened fire. Five men were lined up on the side of the hill and opened fire as they walked forward. Behind them, Jack Wallace pulled his gun but did not fire. Instead, he calmly watched the chaos erupt.

Octavio heard the loud boom of guns and wails from the animals, and a tremble in the earth that he realized was the cattle stampeding away from the noise. Then Reynaldo screamed, a high hissing sound.

Octavio had never heard anything like it. It just went on and on, and when he finally located him in the mess, his face was wrong. The bottom half of his jaw was gone, broken teeth and the black hole of his mouth exposed, throat peppered in black and red. Reynaldo ran until another shot cut off the scream and he fell to the earth. Octavio dove to the ground and pulled Ignacio with him. His childhood friend. Octavio reached for his knife, but his hand was shaking and he couldn't quite get a hold of it. There was so much noise and dust. The ground was wet and as he shook his hand, flecks of blood and grit flew off. Ignacio pulled out his own knife. He hunkered in place, eyes wide. Pedro ran toward them but fell when his left leg was shot off. Pedro, who was only fifteen, who would have been a fine vaquero someday, opened his mouth but didn't scream, his jaw working as more shots opened up his insides and spilled them out.

Octavio finally worked his knife free and wiped his face with the back of his hand. It came back bloody, and he realized a gash was weeping on his cheek from a grazing bullet. His shoulder bloomed with pain as something slammed him to his back. He picked up the knife with his other hand and threw it at the coward who shot him, where it embedded in the man's thigh.

"You shouldn't have done that." The man aimed his rifle.

Octavio knew no more.

5.

A KETTLE OF VULTURES passed overhead, a large dark mass mimicked by its thinner, paler shadow on the ground. Bright pink-red heads with bulbous beaks stuck out from their otherwise sleek bodies, wings spread wide as they soared overhead in ragged harmony. Two black vultures hung back, watching for when the others scented something so that they could swoop in and steal the food.

Mariluz wondered where they were off to, what had died, wishing she could be up there with them. Sweat dripped from her hairline, stinging her eyes as she squinted upward, following them. Concentrating. Trying to remember what Jovita had taught her.

She focused on the rightmost bird, staring at it, trying to see what it saw. To meld with it. To fly as a bird and have only the cares of a bird. To hunt for food rather than to be hunted. To leave whenever she wanted. Jovita told her it took patience and stillness to see through their eyes, something Mariluz had only done once as a child. But she didn't want to just see through their eyes, she wanted to *become* one. Jovita ignored her complaints, told her to keep practicing. So she kept on, though she was more frustrated than ever.

The shadow drifted over some mesquitales a few miles away, having found something dead and rotten enough to eat. Mariluz sighed. Maybe one day she would fly with the birds. But not today.

She had chores to do and work to finish. Clothing to mend and bring back to Eva's Place. Mariluz did the girls' laundry once a week and did some sewing for them as well, mostly mending clothing ripped by rowdy customers but sometimes embroidery as well. Her skill as a seamstress was known, but Eva was the only regular client that she kept. Sometimes Eva felt like family more than her own brother did.

Octavio was off on a cattle drive, not due back for months. So Mariluz took care of his güera wife. Sarah was nice enough, knew enough Spanish to carry on a conversation—and she had good pronunciation, unlike most of the gringos they had met who tended to butcher the words. Together, when it was just the two of them, they spoke a mixture of Spanish and English. Sarah missed speaking English, and her goal was to help Mariluz become fluent so that they could have full conversations in her native language. For now, they were content with the blended form they devised. Having each of them uncomfortable placed them on equal ground. Mariluz was self-conscious, aware of how thick her tongue felt in her mouth when she tried to speak in English, the words inevitably pronounced wrong or in the wrong order.

The children were better at mastering both languages than any of them. The twins, at age five, could speak better English than Mariluz ever would, and without an accent. Another thing to resent them for, bastard children in every way. She rubbed the scar that ran across her left cheek, the deepest scar, the one that always burned when she thought about them. She felt it white hot just as she did when the knife drew across her skin three years ago.

Sarah told her it wasn't their fault and she should love them no matter what. After all, Mariluz was their mother.

But she wasn't, not really. She was the vessel that had carried them, that had been broken open for them, letting them come screaming out into the world. That made her responsible for them. But they weren't hers. They couldn't be, not when she saw *his* eyes looking out of their heads, a strange watery blue that contrasted with their tan skin, eyes that made her shiver when she saw them as though he were looking through them and saw her as though they were as cruel and calculating as he. She might have given birth to them, but they never let her forget where they came from, who they really belonged to.

Mariluz shook her head, the calmness from watching the vultures dissipating. She took one last look, where a faint darkness shimmered in the bright sun. A shadow fell over her, moving to the east. Above her a lone vulture soared, its red head appearing to look down at her. Mariluz looked back, squinting against the sun, as the bird made a lazy circle and then continued away.

She looked at the sky and again wished again for a freedom she could not have. For now Sarah needed her, and so did *they*. The children did small chores, but they still took a lot of care. Care she didn't want to give. The early morning time she took was her only chance at peace and quiet. She looked up again, but the vulture had disappeared. Gone on its way.

Sarah's pregnancy was taxing. Instead of flourishing, her pale skin became even more pale, growing taut, her body thinning as the child grew fat inside her.

It's eating her from the inside.

Mariluz didn't know where the thought came from, but she knew it was right. Sarah should not be pregnant. The child inside of her was a taker. It took and took and took and would continue taking after it was out of her body. If Sarah survived. Jovita could have helped her get rid of it, but Sarah wanted a baby, looked forward to it in a way Mariluz didn't understand. Especially knowing that Octavio may not even be back before it was born. Instead, Sarah and Jovita worked together, sharing and combining herbal remedies that were supposed to ease her pain and make the pregnancy easier. If this was easier, Mariluz hated to think of what it would be like otherwise.

The merciless summer heat didn't help. Even if she moved Sarah outside in the shade of the covered patio, propped on the old chaise Eva had given them, it was simply too hot for her. Nothing seemed to help. The baby clamped down so tightly that Sarah couldn't breathe right. Her breath came in wheezes, with a rattling sound like the baby was sitting on her lungs. Sarah said that the baby was always pushing, but Mariluz knew it was pulling. Pulling Sarah's life right out of her. She kept her thoughts to herself not wanting to worry Sarah. She would do what she could when the baby came, but Mariluz was no expert on babies or healing, though she was learning.

Mariluz worried about what would happen when the baby came. Jovita and Eva would help, but she thought Sarah might need a doctor. What if they had to take her to the hospital at Fort Hope? The hospital was run by Anglo doctors, but they would care for Sarah. She was one of them. But the hospital would be the last resort. The only thing Mariluz could do was try to protect her.

She decided to make a rebozo, stitching it in secret while Sarah slept. She had purchased the cloth and basic threads from José María, the buhonero who passed through Soledad twice a year. Eva helped her get the other thread she needed on her last trip to San Antonio. Scarlet, gold, emerald, and brilliant purple. Colors the traveling peddler didn't carry. She would use it to embroider brilliant flowers and other designs on the plain cloth before sewing the pieces together. She took care to embroider each stitch with calming influences, saying prayers under her breath to La Virgen and to other deities she could not name. To nature itself, perhaps, though in her mind she saw a faceless, shapeless spirit, a sort of benign sombra. She worked complicated knots into her patterns to keep them strong. And as always, she worked vultures into the complex patterns of roses and vines. Vultures for far sight, for protection. Jovita had told her that all vultures were female. That they gave birth to one baby each, each time a girl. They were protectors and cleaners, much like women, only they were free to do it on their own terms.

Should've done the same for myself, Mariluz thought, rubbing her cheek. But somehow, she knew it didn't work that way. Her skill was in protecting others, not herself. At least not that day. She shook off those thoughts before they spiraled into the darkness.

Her scars tingled, and Mariluz rubbed the large one on her cheek. The one that had twisted and raised up as it healed, as though it needed to be seen. The scar that bonded her to Eva forever.

Eva's Place did steady business ever since Fort Hope was established. Despite the war and the skirmishes that followed, she was happy to have their business and had no problem dealing with the bad drunks and the young men away from home for the first time, the white boys who had never seen a dark-skinned woman before and paid for their exocitism. She took their money and listened to their conversations. There were rumors that she'd had an affair with an American general, but she also had good friends in the Mexican army, friends who could benefit from learning what these men knew. The secrets they spilled to the girls they didn't think would understand but whom Eva had trained well. She made a career of information, feeding it back to the Mexican army and later the rebels. She gave the American troops just enough to make them feel as though she were feeding them secrets as well. Enough so that they paid her well. She knew just how much to give and how to protect herself, and her hotel was considered a neutral space. A place where men from both sides came to play faro or monte, to eat and drink and dance with pretty women.

That night Mariluz had stayed late talking with Carolina and Isabel. Octavio was meeting with the former militia members and wouldn't be home until late, anyway. When they were pulled away to dance, Mariluz wrapped her rebozo around her and left out the back door to walk the few miles across the open fields. The darkening sky was a welcome contrast to the brightly lit saloon. She looked at the bands of twinkling stars above her and wondered if she could embroider something like that. Thought of how she might capture the brilliance of the sky, if it was possible. What plants she might use to dye the linen, which type of thread containing just the right shine to make the stars sparkle as they did in the sky.

And then she was grabbed from behind, a large hand covering her mouth as she was lifted off the ground. He dragged her to an old outbuilding that had once held cattle feed. She saw his face when she twisted around. Travis, the soldier who had beaten Manuela nearly to death after paying for a night with her. Manuela had been bruised everywhere, unable to talk or walk for weeks. He had etched deep lines into her face with his knife. She left Soledad soon after.

Mariluz fought even harder once she recognized him, but the hands that held her were large and strong. And she was just a girl, weak and imprisoned by a beast walking around in the skin of a man. She retreated inward, remembering a day when she was a child, the day with her grandmother when they had watched the vultures pick through the decaying carcass of a coyote. Mariluz watched the birds as her grandmother talked, and admired them. The way each bird lined up gracefully and circled in the sky while their sisters picked through the soft flesh, searching for delicacies with every bite. The rotten smell of death on the wind and the meaty smell of the birds themselves. That day was when Mariluz got to fly as a vulture. Her body dropped to the ground as she rose up and grew smaller, felt herself peeking out from inside a form high above, her vision clearer than it had ever been. She saw two tiny people far below, which she realized were her and her grandmother. Lifted by an updraft, she circled down toward the scent of the coyote's rotting body, knowing it was nearly her turn to eat. She was hungry with the anticipation of digging through its soft insides that would be swollen and ripe, ready to be torn into. Could nearly taste the juices that would nurture her, feel herself tearing into the coyote's musculature and ripping away stringy bits of meat. Chewing and savoring those strands of decaying life. Reveling in the flesh around her as she rent it apart. That had been the happiest day of her life, Mariluz and her grandmother soaring in the sky together seeing through the eyes of the birds they so admired.

Mariluz withdrew into the memory so that she didn't feel the bruises and cuts inflicted on her back, her thighs, her breasts. The cuts on her face, the deepest one burning on her left cheek. Branded like cattle.

She waited until he had gone before turning back toward Soledad knowing she could not go home. Not like this. Her brother would think she had done something, said something, to deserve this. That she hadn't fought hard enough. She shambled slowly, each step a stab of pain, reminding her of a story she'd heard about a mermaid who traded her tail for legs, each step bringing searing pain. Why had the mermaid thought that a good trade? Her open wounds felt like a thousand rats gnawing at her skin. She stood tall, willing herself not to show the hurt as she shuffled forward with an awkward gait, refusing to let anyone else see her pain. Her anger kept her going. She focused on movement. One foot, then the next. The light and noise from Eva's emerged as if through a fog over her hearing. Blood pounded in her ears, loud as wild horses running across a plain. She made no attempt to cover herself, letting them all see if they wanted the welts on her breasts, her stomach, the blood running down her skin. It was already starting to crust and dry in various cracks and crevices of her body, leaving a burning itch to accompany the burn of the numerous scrapes and scratches elsewhere on her body. She had to urinate, and that created another burn in her body. The wounds on her face wept slow blood like honey down her cheeks. Each movement was agony, but she held her head up and looked only forward, one foot in front of the other, leaving a trail to Eva's doorway.

The piano player stopped, and the room grew quiet when she walked in. She collapsed only after Osiel, one of Eva's regular customers, carried her to a back room away from the noise. Eva tended to her wounds, doing what she could to repair the damage, letting her sleep in her bed on the softest sheets Mariluz had ever felt. Eva sent someone to fetch Jovita, and she slept on the floor that night, holding Mariluz's hand.

She stayed with Eva for a week, until the worst of

her external wounds had healed with help from herbal compresses and many glasses of foul-tasting tea. When the bruises faded from stormy purplish-black to a vomitous green-yellow and the cuts on her face were outlined with a less vicious red, she walked to the house she shared with her brother and told him what he wanted to hear, that nothing was wrong. She was fine.

Travis had disappeared not long afterward. The sheriff at the time, Don Francisco, did not spend much time looking for him. And if people thought it was odd that he disappeared at the same time three families slaughtered pigs, well, he was sure that was just a coincidence.

Mariluz had a daily reminder. A boy and girl born minutes apart. Mariluz hadn't even named them; she let Sarah do that when they were a year old. Julia and Jorge.

"Children need names," Sarah had said. One of their first conversations.

"Son demonios."

But Sarah couldn't or wouldn't listen. "They're children, not demons. You have to call them something."

"Then you name them."

Sarah loved the twins, which was one reason Mariluz couldn't fully trust her. She tried to give the children to Sarah, told her to take them if she loved them. But Octavio raged, telling her to act like a mother. If she was old enough to have children, she should be able to take care of them. Mariluz was nearly sixteen, a woman. She couldn't just give her children to his new wife. He acted like she was crazy, although Travis happened to disappear the night Octavio and some of the other militia members were slaughtering pigs. That was a matter of principle for him. He still thought that somehow it was her fault. She must have done something, said something, to have brought on the attack. And he did not understand why she wouldn't—couldn't—be their mother.

I should have left them in the desert. A gift for the vultures. Or drowned them in the river.

But she hadn't. Could you blame a demon for being born any more than you could blame a vulture for eating the dead? Mariluz sighed and went back toward the house where she could sit and finish Sarah's dress.

Mariluz directed her thoughts toward happier things, praying for Sarah and her baby to have health and happiness. Love. Praying the child wouldn't kill Sarah just to have its own life. She glanced toward the ofrenda on the far wall decorated with lavender and rosemary, candles, and a small painting of la virgen. A shrine for the parents she didn't remember. Octavio had taken care of her for so long, even when they lived with their tío and his family. She prayed for her brother, also, that he would be safe. The room darkened, the candles throwing flickering shadows on the wall that looked like people running. Another shadow on the floor extended and stretched like a bird feeling its wings.

Mariluz shivered. A storm was coming.

6.

HE HOUSES CROPPED up closer together, and the noise and smell of the city reached Juana before she got to San Antonio. The combined smells of cooking food, manure, and smoke made her stomach grumble. A few men on horses rode by, ignoring her. Their voices hung on the heat of the air. The sky was clear, but she could tell a storm was coming. It was in the air.

"You've had too much time to think." Analisa's voice startled her out of her thoughts.

"You sound like my mother."

"Yeah, well, someone needs to look after you. You don't have to be alone, you know."

Juana, irritated, did not answer. She moved one foot in front of the other and decided to find a place to stay for the night. She would take shelter from the coming storm before moving on.

San Antonio had two large general stores that sold all manner of things. She would stock up on supplies before leaving, but for now she walked around and listened, taking a room at a small rooming house about half a mile from downtown, paying extra to ensure she had the room to herself, and she would take her meals in town.

The humidity increased throughout the day, hanging like a blanket of air, making it difficult to breathe. Juana bathed and wondered why she bothered when it felt like she was coated in more grime afterward. She wandered around taking the measure of the town and its people. They were a mix of white, brown, and black, proper and not. There had been a glut of Germans moving to the area, but she also heard British and Irish accents along with those from the American south and east. This disparate group had converged and lived in uneasy harmony. She heard one woman in a clipped British accent say to her companion, "You can't go out after dark here. It's full of Mexes. They swarm like bugs, and they're even more violent than the Indians!" They looked at Juana. Dressed in men's clothing, her hair freshly shorn, they assumed she was a man. They looked at her with a mix of fear and excitement, and she rewarded them with a slow smile, unsheathing her knife and paring her nails. The two women hurried by, and she laughed, wondering what they would think if they could see Analisa. But she was gone to wherever she went when she got sick of Juana.

The storm moved in near midnight, when Juana was safely back in her room. She kept the window open, wanting fresh air to clear out the staleness embedded in the sheets and walls. Years of unwashed bodies cramped into the tiny space. Tiny mites crawled out of the woodwork after dark, and she listened to their chitinous sounds as they went about their work.

She awoke to dampness. Rain fell in sheets, as though she were under a flowing river. The scars on her palm tingled. She needed to leave, but she couldn't until after the storm. Juana didn't mind riding in the rain, but she couldn't risk getting caught in a torrent. It would be foolish to travel until it was over. All she could do was wait it out and hope it didn't last too long.

The storm was two days of bright streaks of lightning and rolling thunder and thick, heavy rain that felt as though a sluicegate had been lifted. Everything turned soggy. The walls in Juana's room swelled with moisture that sweated out in beads at night, the drip-drip-drip like fingernails tapping incessantly on the walls. At least she had an upper room; water had seeped in through the floorboards downstairs.

The streets turned to small rivers carrying the bloated bodies of dead animals. Juana ventured out and ordered supplies to be put aside for when she was able to leave. She went to a hotel to get some food and a drink. There she could sit and think and soak up information. Most of what she heard was interesting, though not very useful. News of deaths and robberies, people moving in and out of the city. One man told of a wagon train he had found years ago, its inhabitants murdered, and the things he had carted away to sell.

She had given up doing anything except waiting and drinking as the afternoon dragged on and the rain continued to fall. A group of four white men played poker while others looked on. It was obvious that the one in the large black hat was the leader. He was quiet, but the others deferred to him, making sure he had what he needed. Probably cheating to make sure he won. Men like him always won. Juana sat back and sipped a whiskey as she tried to hear what they said over the talking of the crowded bar. Something about rounding up men and cattle, only the cattle had been treated better. The men, all Mexicans, had been killed, then strung up on a tree.

"I bet they're ripe to burst about now."

"Like watermelon left in the sun!" A loud chorus of laughter after that.

In the lull after the laughter a voice could be heard. "Just make sure I get paid for sending them your way." The voice belonged to a man in a dirty brown hat. His coat and boots were dirty, caked with mud. He stood next to a man with a large black moustache, slightly apart from the card players.

The men talked loudly, not caring who heard. Juana pieced together that the card players were Texas Rangers. James Ray, an up-and-coming cattle baron, had paid these men a good sum of money to go after a group of cattle rustlers and make a spectacle of them. It was a set up. They weren't real rustlers, but the Rangers didn't much care. A job was a job, and this one paid well. They'd be no great loss. The other two men were part of a group of ersatz Rangers working farther south where Ray and his partner Lewis Sharp were trying to expand their land holdings. The word Soledad caught Juana's attention. They were buying or stealing the land in that area because of rumors the railroad would be coming through. Taking control of the land now would ensure they had an edge on transporting cotton and whatever else Ray planned on dabbling in. These men just wanted a piece of the action.

When the game ended, the man in the brown hat stepped away from the group with the man in the black hat. They had a brief discussion that ended with the man in the brown hat pocketing a small pile of folded bills. He tipped his hat at the men and glared at Juana before stepping out into the rain. The scar on her hand flared and she stared back, though the brim of his hat hid his features. She knew she'd see him again, but for now she had something to take care of.

The game had broken up and most of the men dispersed. Two of the louder ones headed for a saloon down the street that had dancing women, the others stumbled in their own directions. The man in the black hat stayed at his table staring at the empty glass as though he wished he could climb inside. She went to the bar and bought a bottle of whiskey. Brought it to the table.

"You look like you could use another," she said.

He nodded but didn't look up. "Much obliged."

They sipped in silence and then the man said, "Do you ever wonder how you got where you are? Or why you can't leave?" He laughed. "I'm melancholy tonight. Don't mind me. Name's John Ryder."

"Juan Castillo." The name rolled off her tongue without thought. It was easier when people thought she was a man. "The rain makes everything melancholy. Even tough guys like us."

Ryder laughed, and they began to talk.

Ryder was a Ranger, joined up because he thought it was an honorable thing. He'd help keep law and order. "Things've changed," he said. "More people moving in, more problems. More money changing hands. Don't feel the same's it used to. I've been thinking 'bout hanging up my hat, so to speak." He looked at Juana. "Funny how you can tell things to strangers that you can't otherwise. Just whiskey talk."

Juana kept pouring and let him talk. She listened and laughed, though Jack never noticed her smile didn't reach her eyes as she asked him questions.

The rain ensured no one else was around when they left the bar hours later. Ryder never saw her pull the knife. It cut into him so smoothly that he only realized it after warm blood began to flow out of his stomach and the pain began. She came at him quickly, kicking the side of his knee and stomping his ankle when he fell. She enjoyed the surprised look on his face when he realized what had happened. The man in the bar had been sad, ready to quit, but that didn't excuse the things he had done. The people he had bragged about killing just minutes before. She sliced into him over and over, sliding the knife between each of his fingers to keep him awake.

"Do you know how much pressure it takes to dislodge a man's eyeball?" she asked, holding the knife beneath an eye. She slid it into the space between bone and orb before he could respond. The sounds he made reminded her of an old dog that had been run over by an oxcart when she was a child.

Some boys had come and kicked it for a while before getting bored and leaving. It cried for hours before she was able to sneak out and suffocate it. There would be no such mercy for John Ryder.

She turned her attention back to the wound in his stomach and opened it wider, exposing his insides to the night air.

"It's funny how we all look alike on the inside, eh amigo?"

She reached her hand around and squeezed until he stopped moving. She lifted her head to let the rain wash her face clean and closed her eyes.

7.

OSIEL AND HUGO were on their way into Soledad, walking slowly both because of the heat and because it gave them more time to drink. They were headed to Eva's. She only had a piano player, but it was music. If they were lucky, they might get to dance with the ladies . . . and maybe a bit more. They shared a jug of pulque as they walked, in preparation for the afternoon and evening of drinking and dancing to come.

They were so busy laughing and talking, discussing which of the women they hoped would be there, that they didn't pay attention when the horses drew up. The men were dusty as though they'd been on the road a while.

The gringos' clothes were tinged with sweat and dust, their skin reddened and grimy, the reek of unwashed flesh combined with the tang of bitter sweat and the rich smell of old feces that clung to their undergarments.

"Well, well, well," Avery Gifford said as he approached them. He peered at them beneath the brim of his brown hat. "What do we have here?"

"Hola, amigo," Osiel said, his words slurred. He held the jug out to the men before Hugo could stop him. "¡Tener algo!" He waved the jug toward the man and took a step forward.

"Callate, pendejo." Hugo kicked his friend, keeping his gaze to the ground. Why had they started drinking already? The next thing he knew he was down on the ground with his hands over his ears, blood dripping down his face. A loud high-pitched whine with a dull roaring beneath it filled his head. It was like he had fallen into a cenote and heard the echoes of his fall over and over. The ground around him was wet and littered with ceramic shards. Someone had shot the pulque jug and one of those shards had cut Hugo's face. At least he hoped that's what it was. His friend was still standing there like a burro, too stupid to realize what trouble they were in.

The man who had spoken to them walked over, gun in hand but not pointed at them. Calmly, he whipped his gun-hand across Osiel's face. Hugo watched his friend's skin part into a gash that exposed the dull white of his cheekbone. Hugo, seeing far deeper inside his friend than he cared to, threw up. The milky-white mixture splashed back to his face and onto his clothing. It seemed to go on forever. He hadn't drunk that much, but now he was throwing up foul yellow bile that stuck in his throat like phlegm, burning his sinuses and making his eyes water. He heaved for what felt like forever before stopping. Rather than getting up, he remained on the ground trying not to look at the clotted, frothy mixture in front of him as he tried to spit, to get the foul taste out of his mouth. If only he didn't have to smell the vapors rising in the afternoon heat. He pushed himself back a few inches and bumped the man who had walked behind him.

The Anglos talked and laughed as Hugo's head reeled and he tried not to fall into the mess he had created. The noise in his head had subsided at least, but he still couldn't hear what they were saying. Didn't want to know what they were planning to do next. Let it be a surprise, and let it be over quickly so he could go home and lick his wounds. He didn't think they'd be going to Eva's tonight or picking up any women. He could hold his own in a fight, but not against two armed men. Best to let them get their aggression out and move on. Soledad was still too small for all of them.

Osiel was still reeling from the hit, but he looked over at Hugo and winked before lunging upward with a punch. It caught Avery in the gut, knocking a surprised "Whoof" out of him before propelling him to the ground. Avery put a hand down to push himself up and placed it right in the pool of Hugo's puke. He yanked his hand away and fell back to the ground, twisting his wrist and releasing the gun. Hugo surprised himself by laughing and taking a swing at the mustached man closest to him as Osiel kicked Avery in the side. They might have a chance taking them off guard like this. At least they'd have a good story to tell.

The scuffle went on for a few minutes, Hugo getting in a few good hits before Mustache's fist shot out quick and hard. And then everything turned to pain. Hugo's nose was flat and pulpy, spread across his face. Blood and mucus ran into his mouth as he took small panicked breaths. The front of Hugo's tan shirt was covered in mush from his nose. He staggered back, almost falling.

"I heard we can get up to fifty dollars for an Indian scalp," Avery said. He jerked Hugo's head up. Nose goo spattered Avery's face, but he didn't seem to notice. His shirt was already wet with Hugo's bile. His right fist was dark with Osiel's blood. Osiel lay curled up on the ground.

"They're 'skins, not Injuns." This from the mustached man who had destroyed Hugo's nose. *You really should clean that thing*, Hugo thought. The mustache was thick and long and looked like it had caught every fallen moco and speck of old food this guy had ever had.

Avery nodded. "Who cares? And who the hell can tell anyway? Look at 'im. Who's ever gonna know?" He leaned closer, his voice hushed. He held up Hugo's coarse black hair. "Who's gonna tell? Either way we get somethin'. A few dollars is a few more than we have right now."

Mustache considered this as he shoved a knife into Hugo's stomach and twisted. He looked as though he had all the time in the world, as though he needed all that time to think about what Avery had said. As though he didn't hear Hugo's sobs or feel the globs of snotty blood dripping off Hugo's face and onto his arm. He licked his lips, not noticing or caring they were speckled with blood and grue and the unknown crumbs from his mustache.

"What do you think, boy?" he asked. "Is it enough to kill you or should we make you suffer, too?" He laughed as he continued to turn the knife slowly, ignoring the heaves as Hugo tried to throw up again, swinging at the air with weak fists. Vomit stuck in his esophagus and, unable to breathe, he choked slowly while Mustache continued to twist the knife.

"Money's money," Mustache decided. "And I should be compensated for my pain."

"Take care of it," Avery said to Mustache. He turned away and pulled Osiel up by the hair. Chunks of Hugo's vomit clung to his face. The white-hot burn of Avery's knife splitting his skin and sliding under his hairline roused Osiel, but he wasn't awake for long.

8.

THE BRIGHT MOON, nearly but not quite full, floated in the darkness of the river. Juana gazed at it, not wanting to disturb it by soaking her feet. She sighed and then walked on. The night was still and cool, the air filled with the creaks and chirps of crickets and toads, the chitinous whisper of tiny legs moving through the brittle grass.

"Do you miss it?" Analisa asked.

"Miss what?"

"Home." Her blood dripped softly onto the grass, and Juana knew that if she looked at it the patterns would reveal the boxy shape of the house they grew up in. In her mind she saw the pale stone walls, the wrought iron balconies. The various outbuildings that surrounded it. Laughing with Analisa as they planned adventures. Her brothers' teasing. Pepe looking up with his big eyes. Her mother's looks of reproach. Her father's library. Everything now gone, reduced to rubble.

She shook her head. "No. That was another life." The scar on her hand flared and she fought the urge to take out her knife and hold it. "Do you?"

Analisa stared at the sky and did not answer.

She wished she could take Analisa's hand, that she could warm her up and bring her back to her old self. Her friend was what she missed.

The old woman bent over the animal, back curved into a tight arch as she squatted. Her head was inside the burro's stomach. Juana stopped walking, not wanting to get any closer.

"That's sick." Analisa's mouth pulled back into half a grimace. They listened, fascinated, to the slurping sounds she made before grasping both sides of the animal and pulling herself out, like a birth. She shook her head back and forth to tear off a piece of gristle with her teeth. The crickets had quieted, and the only sounds were the loud smacks she made as she worked to chew the meat. She licked bloody slime off of her fingers before beckoning to Juana.

"Both of you," she said, "come."

Juana did not move immediately. This woman could *see* Analisa?

She jolted forward as Analisa nudged her. "What are you waiting for? We don't want to be disrespectful." Analisa gave the woman her lopsided smile and pushed past Juana. "Thank you, abuela."

It was a dream, of course. Juana had left Pepe a few days ago. She remembered walking away wondering if the vultures would pick his bones clean.

"And I thank you for that," the old woman said. "Many blessings on you."

Juana tried to keep her face from showing the mix of surprise and disgust that she felt. Flecks of matter clung to the old woman's face and the hairs that clung to her balding head. The blood gave her skin a dark sheen. Juana tried not to breathe in the fumes of rot that clung to the old woman, an older scent of decay that clashed with the fresher, meatier rot of the dead animal.

Juana said nothing but stood next to Analisa across from the old woman.

"Thank you for coming," she said. "Soldadera Without Mercy."

Analisa clapped her hands together like a child. "She knows you!" Her eye shone with mischief, and her half-smile grew bigger.

"It's not so strange that someone would know me in my own dream," Juana said. She tried not to see the empty cavities where Pepe's eyes had been, the gaping hole of mouth where most of his tongue had been chewed off. The jagged tear in his stomach, a dark pool of blood seeping out around it.

The old woman shook her head. "It is a dream, but not. We called to each other, and we each answered. But that's not important." The old woman shook herself off, and perched on a rock near the fire.

Analisa went forward and sat at the woman's feet, as she used to do when her mother told stories. Juana remained standing with her arms crossed. The woman produced an earthenware mug of fragrant tea and held it out to Juana.

"Come," she said. "Take this."

Juana found herself taking the mug and sitting down cross-legged. She took a polite sip, surprised at how good it was, how it immediately calmed her. "What do you want?"

The old woman smiled, a terrible movement that cracked her face. Her eyes remained flat. Watchful. Before Juana knew what happened, the old woman grabbed her hand and traced the scarred imprint of the sigils from the knife hilt with her rough fingers. "We are part of the same path, you and I. We hold the same hatred for those who would try to supplant and terrorize us and our way of life. Vengeance is like the devil, attractive at first but very deceptive. The choices you make have impact, so you need to choose wisely."

"You're rambling, vieja. Not making sense."

Analisa slapped Juana on the leg, doing her best to glare with her one eye, the one side of her mouth sloped down into a frown. "Respeto." She crossed herself and addressed the woman. "Forgive her, abuela. She is rough and rude, though she means well."

"I don't mind rudeness, but you must listen. You remind me of a man I knew once whose goal was to create a graveyard just to see it filled with Anglos. You want to kill them, and I need you to do that, but you cannot kill for the sake of killing. The lust for power, whether you recognize it or not, is strong. I need you to help someone else. Someone important to me. I'm not strong enough, and there isn't time to teach her what she needs to know. Her anger is growing, and the signs show that it could be bad. Very bad." The woman picked at her teeth, dislodging something before licking it off of her fingers. "But if her anger could be controlled, focused . . . well. She could be more powerful than she knows."

"You want me to control her?"

"No, mija. You misunderstand. She wants to kill

the Anglos and she can't do it alone. She needs to know that she is not alone." Her voice broke and she sounded frail, human for the first time. Her body seemed to lose vibrancy, to fade, and Juana realized she could see through her.

The old woman started to say something and then disappeared.

Juana blinked and found herself back in her bedroll. The night was cool. She fell back asleep and dreamed of Padre Trujillo, her mother's priest. In her dream, he stood in a room yelling at her, though she could not hear his words. His face was flushed, eyes narrowed as he yelled silently. He held up his hands as if to motion her to stop. Behind him in the corner, a woman in blue held her face in her hands and wept.

She headed south in the morning, toward Soledad.

9.

STARS AND A NEARLY full moon lit the dark plains enough to show shadow shapes on the land. Lumps that were mesquite trees, short, stocky blobs of cactus, the edges of the grass and occasional clump of a small bush. The sere grass rustled in whispers that passed from blade to blade. Mariluz could not understand what the grass was trying to say as its messages passed around her. The wind was warm against her face, like the soft hand of her mother. She had almost forgotten what her mother looked like, that she had ever lived with such a person. It had been she and Octavio for so long now, taking care of each other.

The land wasn't familiar. Just plains of sere grass and dirt, the mesquite trees that seemed to creep into different places when she didn't look directly at them. She pressed on, unsure of what she would find or where she was going. The moon and stars shifted position in their usual slow way, but she kept going in what she thought was a straight line, certain she would get where she needed to be eventually—even if she didn't know what or where that place was. After a time, she heard a noise. A soft groan and a rustle. Her heart pounded, and she stopped where she was. Listening and trying to still the feeling of her heart pulsing against her throat.

Something impelled her forward. She stepped lightly, one foot in front of the other through the whispering grass until another shape emerged from the dark. A blob larger and darker than the others she'd passed. Cold darkness that made her want to turn around and run. She had never felt the urge she had now, to turn and flee, to pretend she hadn't seen the shape. That she was not drawn to it. That it had not been there before.

A tree emerged as she drew closer. Coldness enveloped her, freezing her feet in place as she made out the wrongness of their shapes. The stronger limbs were weighted down with large objects.

The sight reminded her of something she had seen as a child. Tío Jorge had taken Mariluz and Octavio with him to visit some Anglo ranchers who had bought property that he owned in the north. It was a long drive, and hot. They were covered in dust that the oxen kicked up. It mixed with the sweat rolling down their faces and bodies, pooling in the cracks and crevices of their skin. They hadn't gone a mile up the faintly worn path leading to the ranch when the wind brought a smell. This was worse than when the oxen let loose their too frequent loads. An overpowering stench that made her eyes water and her throat want to close. Her stomach tightened into a knot that clenched and unclenched like a fist. They crested a small hill that sloped down and to the right, and then she saw it.

Coyotes hung like leaves on an otherwise barren tree, their tails knotted around the limbs. They were packed tightly on the branches, bodies touching. They had hung long enough that their bodies had elongated, skin stretched taut, some with mouths open into eternal, unheard screams. Bluebottle flies clustered on dark spots of dried blood, swarming onto and into the openings where bullets had torn through them. The coyotes on the lowest branches looked like they were reaching for the ground trying to gain traction to run away. But it was obvious that even those whose eyes remained open were dead. Mariluz could not look away, even as she tried not to swallow the noxious odor. She had to look, to imprint this horror on her mind. There were so many. How had they done this? *Who* had done this? Why?

She wondered how the tree still stood, the thin branches not breaking or even bending. There were so many of them. She couldn't count how many there were, this tree made of dead and rotting coyotes. Some of their skins had started to slough off. She wondered how long it would take and what would happen when they did. Would the bones fall out of their open mouths or would the skin split open, spewing whatever remained inside? Perhaps it would become a skeleton tree made of dangling bones like the tree in front of the bruja's house. She jumped out of the cart and threw up, horrified that the smell of her rancid vomit was better than that of the coyote tree.

Her uncle laughed. "Ay, mija. Así es la vida." She wanted to look away, to close her eyes, but she knew her uncle was right. This was the way things were, and she needed to know that. So that she didn't become the coyote.

"It's a cleansing," her tío explained. "They need to show the animals who the land belongs to. They can't have them killing the chickens or livestock. It's their livelihood."

Octavio's hand gripped hers tight with an anger she had never seen in him before. "This is *not* the way things should be. What did they do? They lived the only way they knew how. You never did this to the animals!"

Her uncle didn't bother to answer, merely picked Mariluz up and started the oxen moving again.

"You're too little to understand."

Octavio shook his head. "And they call us savages. There's a difference between killing something because you have to and this."

Her brother's voice echoed in her head along with the memory of the coyotes as she realized the savages had struck again. But this time coyotes were not the victims.

The vaqueros hung from their own ropes, packed side by side, a gruesome imitation of that long-ago scene. They hung close enough that their clothes rubbed against each other in the breeze, making the rustling sound she'd heard earlier. The groan sounded again, and she examined the tree's ghastly decorations. She wondered if the groan was from one of the men, if someone was somehow still alive. No, like the coyotes, these men had been killed before they were hanged. One had a hole in his abdomen from which dark fluid had seeped. His face ended where his jaw had been blown off. Several were missing parts of arms and legs. Their clothing and skin was spattered with dried blood. She turned her attention to the man dangling from the branch on the other side of the tree, and her mouth opened. She knew him. Ignacio, Octavio's friend and partner in the militia. The man who had invited him to drive the cattle. A man whom Mariluz had known as a child and watched grow up. One who she was sure helped her brother feed Travis to the pigs.

Now he hung from this tree, left thigh torn open. A hole had gouged through the leg muscle leaving a gaping cavity. Mariluz breathed in slowly and looked at the man next to him. The man whose face was blackened with blood and grit, whose mouth was a gaping wound of shattered bone and teeth, skin splayed back to show a dark wound where his nose had been. Upper teeth gone except for a molar in the back, lower teeth surprisingly untouched, lower jaw slack giving his face a surprised look. His faded bandana had been replaced by the rough rope that dug into his flesh making it bulge out on either side as it took the weight of his body. The man whose wife would soon have a baby and who waited for him back home. Octavio.

She heard his voice, an echo from long ago. "And they call us savages." The tree a celebration of their triumph over people they thought lower than animals. Mariluz realized the cattle drive had been a set up the entire time. Sarah would never see the money owed to Octavio. They'd explain his death somehow. Soon, men would come and take their house, their land, to be given to the gringos. She had never been this angry before.

And then the groan came again, a loud creak she realized came from the tree itself as though it raged with her. Its limbs were weakening under the combined weight of the men, twelve in total, suspended from the tree. They would soon fall into the pools of blood that had formed below them, left to the wilderness like animals.

The horizon cracked open to show a glimpse of lighter blue, la luz en lo oscura. Mariluz felt a tug in her stomach, a string calling her back. Only then did she realize why she didn't know where she was or how she got there. She hadn't really been there. Not her body, anyway.

It was still dark when she woke up in her own bed, warm tears flowing down her cheeks, still hearing the sound of the tree creaking under the weight of her brother and his compadres.

10.

THE MEN STORMED into Jovita's jacal when the stars were still visible, the ground wet with dew, expecting to catch her unaware. But there she stood in the middle of the floor, propped up by her ever-present stick.

"I suppose you know why we're here," Avery said. "Will you go quietly?" He looked at Carlos and waited for him to translate.

"I know why you're here, and I will not leave my house." Jovita replied.

Carlos wanted to plead with her, to tell her what had happened to the others who had refused. But he had a feeling she already knew. She knew more than she should, living way out here and never venturing into Soledad. She had even known that they were coming. Instead, he repeated what she said for Avery.

"Then you'd best hand over the deed or the money." Avery grinned knowing she had neither.

She merely stared at him.

Avery smiled as though that was the answer he had hoped for. That smile let the others know that it was time.

"Please," Carlos begged her. "Just do what they say. You don't want this!" She looked at him and raised one thin eyebrow.

"Hey!" Avery turned steely eyes toward Carlos. "You don't speak except what I tell you to." He gestured, and Valentine shot his fist out, punching Carlos in his previously injured cheek.

Carlos quickly looked down as his eyes watered, not wanting to see what happened next. Not wanting to be a part of it. He turned to Avery. "We should be careful. She was the one who drove out the Guajardo rancheros for Mr. Cavazos. She cursed their cattle and killed them. She cursed the family, too, so that Cavazos could take over their land. Their blood dried up in their bodies, and when they were found, they dumped the blood out of their skin like sand. She can do things—"

Avery held a hand up. "You believe that? I don't believe this old bird can do much of anything 'cept scare people. But if she did, she probably went over and poisoned them. Weren't no curse." He scoffed, but a part of him reluctantly admired her. Someone like that could be useful. It was almost a pity she'd have to go, but look at her. Even if she had powers, she was far too wretched to be much good now. All she lived on was these stories about her that probably happened—*if* they ever did—a hundred years ago. They were doing her a favor, really. Putting her where she should have been long ago: out of her misery.

As Avery moved toward her, Jovita kept her eyes on Carlos. In perfect English she said, "Juan Carlos, you didn't mind coming to me when you got the little Mendoza girl in trouble a few years ago. Is she still *your girl*? Does she know what you put into her pulque that night? That you were responsible for the aches and pains and the bloody mess that almost killed her? But, of course, she was only good for what you wanted, and after you got rid of the child you also got rid of her." She sighed at the look on his face and shook her head.

Benny hooted and clapped Carlos on the back. "Didn't know you had it in you!"

Jovita continued. "You really thought I didn't know? Of course I knew. She would never ask you to do such a thing, no matter what you told me. And now you will get rid of me, because you see women as only something to use." She looked at each of the men in turn. "You all do."

Simon bared his teeth. Benny slapped Carlos on the back and laughed again.

"Shut her up," Avery said and hocked a large wad of phlegm on the floor.

Joe stepped forward. He grabbed Jovita's arm, and she immediately flung it away. Her skin felt like paper, thin and dry. But it was also warmer than it should be and he had the feeling his hands might sink into that skin and never come out again. But he knew he had to do it and reached out again.

Jovita bent forward, a dark rainbow with arthritic hands and feet. Her toes dug into the dirt floor, and she gripped the bastón tightly while muttering to herself.

Benny wrenched the stick out of her grip and laughed as she fell to her knees. He kicked her in the kidney, knocking her over. And then all she saw was boots and her own stick being used as a club to beat her about the face. Her remaining teeth scraped delicate tissue as they tore from her gums. They eased out of her mouth slowly, caught in her bloody drool. Loud screeches interrupted the soft murmur of her voice, the physical pain making her body react. Blood fell from her scalp as thin ropes of hair came loose. The incantation she had been murmuring dulled the pain, but it didn't prevent her body from curling up even more or the blood from flowing. Her clothes, already ragged, fluttered with the wind from the men's movements as they sought to stomp her out of existence. She flinched involuntarily, screeches fading, as she continued to chant, blood now seeping from her mouth in thick strands, covering her skin like mud. Carlos stayed back at first, but after a few mocking words from Avery, he joined in, seeming to draw further anger each time he connected with Jovita's body, trying to erase the shame of her words by erasing her. With each kick he felt her thin body resist. She should have been dead already. He kicked out, wanting to feel her bird bones snap. His mother's face, disappointed, came into his mind and he kicked out even harder trying to make her image go away. Not wanting to think of his mother and what she would have said if she'd seen him like this. Not wanting to see himself. The men tore into her as though she alone had been responsible for some evil that was done to them.

But she hadn't done anything to them . . . yet.

That would come later, when it was time. Just as she knew that this was her fate. To be kicked and beaten by these dirty, stupid men who thought they could own the land as they tried to own people.

Valentine pulled out a knife, a cuchilla he had stolen from a peasant farmer farther south. The peasant had been stabbed to death with it for doing nothing more than cultivating his crops with a knife this man felt should be his. Jovita saw this as she looked at the man stabbing into her, slashing indiscriminately. She had become a creature of dark blood. If she had been an animal she would have crawled away to die in a hole. Her small frame moved up and down, breath coming in jagged pants as she blinked blood out of her eyes, mouth still moving, forming the silent words that kept her going.

She felt little pain, but she heard the snap and felt her arm go loose when they kicked her shoulder out of its socket. Heard her hips snap with a crunch like stepping on a roach, felt her ribs curl inward except for two that poked out of her skin. It was nearly done. She was glad that her strength surprised and infuriated them. They had expected a little old woman who could be beaten into submission, a savage they could tame. But that had never been her way.

Avery was saying something, but she couldn't hear, couldn't understand. She just continued to stare at him as she mouthed her words. It was almost over. He had already been cursed, but he didn't know it yet. Too mean, too dumb to see that this was his own grave being dug while she would be set free. She laughed even though it hurt, the sound coming out of her like a moan. She ignored Avery's demands that she shut up, stop talking.

Valentine and Joe held her down while Avery cut out her tongue. It took longer than it should have since her mouth was already slick with blood from her battered gums and cheeks. She stared at him the entire time, her beady black eyes focused on his face. He concentrated on her eyes next, using his hands to claw them out, hoping it hurt. But her mouth continued to move weakly. She just wouldn't quit.

Avery dragged her out of the house as the sun tore open the sky and stained it crimson; her arm felt as though it might break free from her body, and she wondered if he would club her with it if given the chance. He gave her a sharp look when a soft cackle escaped her but continued to drag her along.

"This ain't right," Valentine said. "She shouldn't be laughing. She should be dead." His face paled, and she laughed again.

"Maybe she is a witch," Simon said and adjusted his hat with a bloodied hand. "Maybe we should—"

"It's fine," Avery said. "A trick. She wants us to think she's not hurt."

But Carlos shook his head. "We shouldn't have done this," he said. *Nagual*, he thought, panicked. He wondered why she hadn't changed into whatever monster she became and escaped.

"It's a little late now, ain't it?" Avery pulled Jovita harder. She gave a muffled "uumph." "She's dead already. She just don't know it yet. But she will."

His smile froze Carlos in place. *Avery might be even crazier than she is*, he thought. He wished he had listened to his mother when she told him to stay away from the gringos.

Jovita lay near the river, nothing more than a limp piece of bloodied flesh and scraps of cloth. The men gathered fallen branches to stack around her. An idea befitting a witch. Avery's first idea had been to burn her in the house so they could start fresh, but there was too much chance of the trees catching fire. And he wanted those trees for the new house that would be built there. A real house with two stories, white walls, and glass in the windows and all those trees to protect it from the merciless sun. Avery's eyes were pools of hate and triumph. The smile continued after he lit the match that kindled the flames.

As her body burned, sending up smoldering dark smoke while bone separated from charred skin, a kettle of vultures soared overhead. Ashes containing bits of Jovita Flores danced in the air before falling into the river and mixing with the sandy grit on its banks, her body returning to the earth from whence she'd come.

A breeze blew, running through the men's hair like a lover's soft fingers promising more to come. Above them, the vultures looked down as if to memorize who they were. Avery's smile faltered.

11.

THAT NIGHT HE stayed in while the boys were off celebrating, blowing off steam. The oil lamp burned low on the table, and Avery leaned back in his chair and closed his eyes. Opened them. They'd celebrated as they always did by drinking too much and getting rowdy, picking a fight that quickly got out of hand. No matter how much he drank, he couldn't get a buzz going. Whiskey just sat in his stomach, making him queasy. He'd spent over an hour in the outhouse sweating like a black dog in the middle of summer as the acidic warmth oozed and wormed its way out of his rectum and into the already stinking pit. The mud-like, blood-streaked stream just went on and on, making his ass nearly as sore as the blisters on his face. It was too fucking hot down here, but it would be worth it. He knew it would. He'd finish up this job for Ray and become sheriff of this little shitting town. He'd control it the right way. It'd be civilized. He'd be in charge with his pick of the women who moved in and a share of the profits from the railroad. Yes sir, the good life lay just ahead.

The oil lamp threw shadows on the wall, seeming to be in constant movement, but the night was quiet. It would stay that way until the boys came back, and he relished the silence. He left the lamp lit and climbed up on his bunk. A gauzy spider web formed a triangular trap in the corner. He brushed his arm out to sweep it away and noticed too late that the shadow was actually a cluster of tiny baby spiders huddling together as though still in their egg sac. They shot out in panic, covering him in filmy wisps and moving legs. It tickled where they ran across his skin. He tried to slap them away, but that only sent them scurrying onto his face, in his hair, down his chest and legs. He let out a loud moan as he tried to shake them off, and then he felt it on his arm. The slower creeping of eight legs that had weight to them. The dark shape crawled up his arm. He flung it up, smacking his hand into the ceiling, rolling off the bunk, and slamming his back on the floor as the spider bit into him. As he fell, a shadow danced on the wall. The haggard brown face of the Mexican witch appeared above him. It couldn't be her. He'd watched her burn, not leaving until the ashes stopped falling. But there she was, leaning over him, stump of a tongue wagging as though she were about to kiss him.

When he came to, the spiders and the witch were gone. All he had was a lump on the back of his head and a raised-up welt on his arm where the big spider had bit him. It was sensitive to the touch, swelled into a hard, round lump. He tried sucking out the poison, but there was no entry point, no bite marks, just the bump. All his efforts did was make it swell up even more and bring tears to his eyes.

He decided to spend the night with Mae Beth. She wouldn't ask any questions.

Mae Beth's massage did what he hoped. Got his mind off the whopper of a dream he'd had earlier. Of course it had been a dream. That old hag was not a witch and she hadn't cursed him. He had drank too much and gotten sick, that's all. It was a fever dream. And now, here with Mae Beth, it started to fade away. There was nothing but her touch on his back and then the feel of her mouth on his skin, the warmth as she straddled him. He kneaded her breasts and drew her down to him so he could touch her silky blonde hair and taste her strawberry lips. He opened his eyes and saw her toothless mouth open in a parody of ecstasy, broken piece of tongue waggling in the back of her mouth as she leaned over him, the screech of her laughter. Her claws dug into his shoulders and he heard Mae Beth's voice say, "What's the matter, baby? Aren't you enjoying it?" He screamed and tried to push her off, but she held on like a rider trying to tame a wild horse.

Jovita continued to laugh, holding him with thin arms as strong as any man's. Somehow he was still inside of her. "Git offa me, bitch!" He wrenched his arms free and grabbed her by the throat. Felt her claws rake his face and his upper arms, drawing downward until they hit the raised bump of the spider bite. The pain almost made him let go, so he squeezed harder, trying to wipe the smile off of her face. To kill her for good this time. She struggled for breath, her hits getting weaker. She clutched his arms, her nails digging into the raised lump of the spider bite. He yelled as he pushed with all his might, flinging her off of him at last. The smack of her head as it hit the wood was lost in his agony and the realization that hundreds of tiny spiders were now crawling out of his arm. He screamed and flailed, trying to knock them away, finally grabbing his knife and digging into his skin to try and get them out. More swarmed out the deeper he went, and he wiggled the knife around trying to get every last one. At last, they were gone, spinning their floating webs that carried them to the bed, the ground. Blood and green-yellow pus seeped out of his arm, and he tore off a piece of the dirty sheet to wrap it.

Mae Beth lay against the wall, blood trickling from her nose and ears, Avery's handprints visible on her face and neck, blue eyes gazing sightlessly at the ceiling.

SARAH WAS UP EARLY, wanting to talk, not realizing anything was wrong. Her color was back along with her energy. They took a short walk to the river, Sarah lumbering along next to Mariluz as she scanned the sky for vultures, Julia and Jorge running ahead and then circling back to them. Mariluz could not speak, knowing she had to tell Sarah that her husband would not be coming home. That not only had he died but what they did to him afterward. To him and his friends. She let Sarah do the talking and focused on picking wildflowers and herbs that grew wild, pointing out the spots where javelina had fed on the cacti and lechuguilla.

"Things are looking up, hermana," Sarah said. "I told you—nothing can be that bad for that long. Soon Octavio will be back, and we'll be a family again." She rubbed her stomach for emphasis and smiled, looking for all the world like a painting of la virgen come to life.

The river was high from the recent rain, and the children splashed in it, laughing and running.

Mariluz swallowed and blinked, trying to gain

control of her emotions. She could not—*would not*—tell Sarah about Octavio. Maybe it had just been a bad dream. Just because she dreamed it did not mean it was truth. But somewhere deep inside, Mariluz knew her brother and his friends were dead and that others would follow. She tried not to show the anger that was growing inside her against the people who would do such things. She focused instead on the beauty of the day.

Eva was waiting outside the house when they got back. Her hair and clothes were mussed from the ride, but she didn't seem to notice. She waved when they came within view, beckoning them to move faster. Mariluz kept them at a slower pace, partly because she saw Sarah had begun to wince when she took a step and partly because she wanted to keep the false peace she had cultivated as long as possible. Nothing that brought Eva over so early in such a state could be good. They sent the children off to play before going inside with Eva.

Jovita was gone. Mariluz tried to digest the news, but it didn't make sense. She was old, yes, but she had always been old. She couldn't be gone, would be around forever. Certainly not burned to a crisp. She shook her head back and forth and sat on the ground like a child, face in her hands, not crying.

She refused to cry. Not now. Instead, she went out back to the kitchen to make mint tea. Tea made everything better, or so she once thought. Jovita had a tea for every ailment, it seemed, but Mariluz had not learned them all yet. *Focus*, she told herself. *Tears are useless. They do nothing and solve nothing.* She stood tall and walked back into the house, keeping the tray with the teapot and cups still so they did not clack together. Sarah would be pleased.

But Sarah did not care about the tea. She looked ill after they told her what had happened.

"Why would they do that? And to burn her?"

"Why do they do anything?" Eva threw her hands up. "If you don't believe me, go see for yourself. You'll smell her. I can't believe they did it. I just can't believe she's gone." She took a cup from the tray and thanked Mariluz.

Sarah excused herself and lumbered slowly outside, probably to the outhouse. Mariluz would have helped her, but today she was numb. It felt like she was seeing everything through a fog. Her movements and thoughts were delayed. Once again, she wished she was a bird and could just fly away, forget these human emotions that hurt so much and kept her here. "Octavio is gone, too," she heard herself say.

"What?" Tea sloshed into the saucer Eva held beneath her cup. She set both on the ground and looked at Mariluz. "What do you mean he's gone?"

Mariluz set her cup and saucer on the tray and told Eva about her dream. "I don't know how I know, but it wasn't just a dream. I *saw* them. Saw him. My brother and the others. How can I tell Sarah? And the rest of their families? They'll all think I'm crazy or . . . " she let the last part trail off. They would blame her for not being able to stop it.

Eva opened her mouth to speak, but Sarah spoke before she could. She must have crept in while they were talking. "I believe you," she said in a soft voice. She looked like a scarecrow, thin arms and legs sticking out beneath her billowing dress, new rebozo atop it, hair pulled back into loose braids. She sat next to Mariluz and held her hand tightly. "I wish I didn't." Sarah's shoulders shook as she cried.

I'm so sorry. I didn't want you to know. Mariluz could not look at Sarah.

"I also believe you. Jovita told me you had more gifts than you knew. That's why she chose to teach you." Eva sipped her tea. "Don't look so surprised. She was my grandmother's sister. I've known her all my life, and she was like a mother to me. Just like she was to you."

Mariluz could not speak. Words caught in her throat and scratched it, making her cough. She wanted to wail and cry or screech. She realized she had been hoping they would call her a liar and tell her it wasn't true. Do something to prove that her brother and mentor were still alive. She would wake up and find it had been a cruel joke or a bad dream. But for them to believe frightened her. She didn't want this responsibility.

"I don't want it," she said. "What good is it to know and not be able to stop it? To not *do* anything?" Her voice grew into a shout. She closed her mouth, not wanting the children to hear.

Eva came over and patted her hand. The closeness of Sarah and Eva, even though she liked—no, loved—both of them, was stifling. She couldn't breathe and pushed them away.

"Would you rather not know? How cruel would that be to wait and wait for someone who never came home?" Eva had gone back to her perch on the small settee. She looked annoyed. "You have knowledge.

You can do something. You can prepare and plan and be ready for whatever comes next. I'll have to tell their families. I can say that I heard about it at the hotel. That way no one else has to know."

Sarah rubbed her protuding stomach. She smiled, but her face was pallid. "We will figure it out, Mariluz. Whatever happens, we will stay together . . . if you want."

But Mariluz had retreated inward, wondering how birds felt when one of their kind was slain. If they felt anything at all or if they were as empty as she was at that moment.

The hooting of an owl woke Mariluz late at night. Angry tears welled up in her eyes as she remembered the day, and she fought them back as she quietly slipped on her huaraches and crept outside. She felt pent up, like an animal. There was nowhere to go now that Jovita was dead.

It was too much to lose Jovita and her brother so close together. *It wasn't fair!* They hadn't done anything to those men, the ones who murdered Jovita or the ones who murdered Octavio. She felt she might explode with rage and grief. How could people stand it? Her parents had died before she was old enough to miss them, and her uncle had been kind but distant. When he left for Louisiana, it was no real surprise that she and Octavio had been left behind. They belonged here. To the land and the people who loved it, like Jovita. She should have died a natural death. Not killed at the hands of mere men. Octavio should have been able to meet his child. To raise it as he had raised Mariluz. Not always perfect but there. What would Sarah do? Would she take the baby and leave? She had said they would stay together, but why should she? There was nothing to keep her here once the baby was born.

Another panicky thought. *What about Julia and Jorge?* How would she take care of them if Sarah left? Surely, it was only a matter of time before she moved on. Everybody else had gone, why should Sarah be any different?

Mariluz walked until the sun came up, but she could not walk off her grief. Or her fear.

Sarah's labor pains started just before midday; she would give birth soon. *Not now. It's too soon.* Mariluz tried not to panic, focused on sensible things like fetching water and holding Sarah's hand.

Jovita was not here to help. She'd have to help Sarah herself.

Something's wrong.

"Something's wrong, Mamá!" Julia's blue-grey eyes were wide, scared. Sarah lay on the bed with her eyes squeezed shut. Blood stained her dress and the mattress, bright and red.

Mariluz remembered her own labor, the gush of fluid and pain that accompanied it. But not thick blood. Not like this. Instead of the quick surge of watery fluid, this was a slow seepage that showed no sign of stopping. Mariluz felt lost. The compress she had made would slow the bleeding but not stop it. They needed help.

"Run and fetch Eva, mijita. Take Jorge with you.

Tell her . . . tell her to come quick!" The girl hugged Mariluz's leg, and Mariluz hugged her back. Without thinking, she kissed the girl on the head and sent her on her way. *Please,* she thought. *Please help her.*

That evening, Sarah lay on her bed atop a fresh sheet, baby in her arms. Mariluz had carefully washed away the blood and mess and dressed Sarah in a clean nightgown. Her skin looked too pale against the soft pink material and the shock of black hair on the baby's head.

Eva put her hands on Mariluz's shoulders and squeezed. "Let them rest."

Mariluz let herself be led away, certain this was yet another dream. She had tried so hard, whispering protective spells, coaxing Sarah, doing all she could think to do for her. But the baby had been turned the wrong way, the cord wrapped around his little neck. And the blood seemed to pour out of Sarah. He had been too much for her after all.

Mariluz would not allow herself to cry, to believe this was real.

Eva had arrived as quickly as she could, leaving Carolina to watch them until she returned. It had been quicker for her to ride out alone. Eva and Mariluz had managed to turn the child and ease him out, but he never took a breath. He had died along with his mother, or perhaps before.

Now they sat outside holding cups of cool tea. It was still hot, the sun not yet set, but felt to Mariluz as though night had already fallen and it would be a long time before daylight came again.

Eva sipped her tea and stared at the rosemary plant near the corner of the house. "There are rumors that the gringos are trying to take over Soledad. They want to move us out. That's nothing new, I know. But they're taking action now. You know what happened to Jovita, and more people are . . . disappearing or being killed. Just the other day, two men were beaten to death. Osiel and Hugo. They were borrachos, but they were harmless. Some people may have moved, but others are just . . . gone." Her voice cracked. "We are at war whether we like it or not. You and the chiquitos should go."

Mariluz laughed but did not answer. tared at the sky while thoughts ran through her head, rubbing her scarred face. Go where? To what? How would they survive? She had no money, and it wouldn't feel right to take the little that Sarah had, even if she had no other family. When it was all of them together, it made sense to move. But how could she make it alone?

"And you?" she heard herself asking. Her voice was rough as though she'd been sick. "What will you do, Eva? Continue to profit from the 'news' you like to gather? Continue reaping the profits while the rest of us die?"

"That *information* has helped us more than you know. I don't answer to you or to anyone. I'll ignore your accusations for now. All I can say is that I would have helped if I'd known what happened. You know me well enough to know that. But you're upset, so say what you need to."

Mariluz sighed and continued to watch the sun melt into the horizon. She welcomed the grief that came with knowing the people she loved best were now dead. Jovita, Octavio, Sarah. But beneath the grief, something else. A glimmer of anger that people should get away with the things that were done to Jovita, to Octavio. That someone as kind as Sarah would be taken away so senselessly. She remembered hearing about heaven and hell when she was a child, a priest who had come through and held services once a month. She thought now that the priest had it wrong. They were already in hell and sought a way out. She wondered what had happened to that priest. If he had found the salvation he went on and on about.

Eva stayed the night, telling Mariluz they would go to town in the morning to get the children and make arrangements to bury Sarah and the baby.

After hours of sitting on a chair staring at the wall, Mariluz arose. Full of want and longing and rage, she walked the few miles to Jovita's house without noticing where she was, not seeing the stars or moon illuminating the sky, paying no attention to the creatures in the grass, not seeing the dark shape perched on the roof of Jovita's jacal.

The door to the house hung open. She almost hoped the men who did this were in there. She had no weapons and did not know how to fight, but hatred simmered within that anger, and that hatred would fuel her to fight them. A fight to the death would be merciful. She felt a tingling, a power similar to but *more* than what she felt when she sewed her little spells into the clothing. Spells that didn't seem to do much good. *This* was what Jovita should have taught her, how to channel her rage and use of it. It felt . . . good.

She smiled a cold, vacant smile as she entered Jovita's house and lit a small lantern on the floor. The smile remained even as she saw the mess they had made. Jovita's belongings were strewn across the floor, broken glass and straw everywhere. The blanket Mariluz made for her had been slashed, the carefully stitched vultures and flowers reduced to jagged threads. She thought of the money she had spent to buy the materials, the hours of work put into getting it just right. Gone to tatters now, and its magic with it. If there ever was any. Eva had helped her get the materials so it would be perfect. Eva. She should have been kinder to Eva. But it was too late for that. The cold smile tightened as Mariluz gritted her teeth. None of that mattered now.

Octavio, Jovita, Ignacio, Felix, Pedro, Joseph, Luís, Hugo, Osiel. She said their names over and over in her head until her anger was a red-hot light behind her eyes. Jovita's rebozo had been stomped into the dirt floor, but it was still intact. Mariluz shook it out and wrapped herself in it, stroking the worn feathers woven into it. Vultures' feathers. Their texture calmed her as her anger grew. She closed her eyes, opened them. Took a breath in and another out. It was no use fighting her anger any more than it was to fight the grief she felt when she realized Sarah was dead. Grief was useless, selfish even. But anger could be useful. She reveled in it. Willed her body and mind open to it, welcomed all of the anger that filled the land and people around her. Years of stored up rage filling her until her skin swelled, grew taut.

Small cracks appeared in the tight places between her fingers and toes as talons poked through. Blood beaded in her pores as they expanded. The scar on her face burned, set aflame once again as the scar tissue pushed outward. Her bones cracked as she arched her back in pain. She felt every inch of her body being crowded out by the rage she had swallowed. Just for a second she thought about Jorge and Julia. That brought with it another type of anger. She gave in, letting it consume her, letting it take away the body she hated, the pain she carried for years, the responsibilities she didn't want.

Her lips cracked as she opened them to release her rage, but her yell turned to a cry of agony. Her skin was stretched to the limit, and tiny, sharp quills poked through her skin. The scar on her face was aflame. She clawed at it, but her hands wouldn't work right, and then she fell to the floor and curled up like a child. She could not scream; her throat did not work. Her scar flared up again as it slit open from the inside and a sharp beak poked out. She felt her bones crack, shattered by the new shape inside of her. Her face seemed to fall in on itself even as her skin broke open. The tickling sensation from the soft fuzz of feathers was lost in the pain of her human body splitting open to let her true self out. She fell into darkness amidst the crack and crunch and tearing of her birth.

13.

THE RUTTED TRACK that led into Soledad was empty, and Juana stopped her horse. She was tired, had been riding most of the night, a nagging feeling that she was too late, driving her to go ever faster. The going hadn't been easy with all of the flooding and debris. Rivers the color of the chocolate Tía Carmen used to make roiled and rushed along. She remembered how excited they had gotten as children when she came and made her special chocolate drink with just the right amount of chile, she and Analisa all smiles with wet brown moustaches. She hadn't thought of Tía Carmen in years and wondered if she was still alive. But she belonged to another life, there was no time for that. Clouds of insects swarmed, drawn to the moisture and the swollen, rotting bodies of possums and raccoons. Two days out they had come upon a wake of vultures feeding on a dead coyote, tearing its soft body apart with their beaks, greedily gulping down the soft meat. She was reminded of the old woman in her dream, the way she had savored the burro's remains. From that point on, a vulture flew ahead of them in the sky, leading them around the worst of the flooding. Juana fell into an exhausted sleep each night, without dreams, and Analisa remained silent. There was nothing to talk about. But this morning she awoke after sleeping for just a few hours, long enough for the horse to rest, and then pushed on through the night.

The heat beat down on Juana, and she wanted to lay down. To find a river and bathe until she felt clean again. Instead, she kept going. That nagging feeling was getting worse. She turned her bandana around to give the nape of her neck extra protection, but beneath the heat she was cold.

"Look," Analisa said, turning her eye up to the sky. Their guide vulture caught a current of air and circled higher and higher, wings spread wide forming a small v-shape. It circled over a cluster of trees about half a mile away.

Juana turned the horse and headed for the trees, hoping she'd find whatever she was meant to find before it was too late—but she was afraid they'd already run out of time.

The door of the tiny jacal hung loosely open, and Juana stepped inside. The sigils on her palm began to burn as she reached for her knife. "Ay!" she cried, as it seared her skin, releasing her grip on the knife.

A vulture jumped up in fright, spreading its wings. Wet fluid glistened on its reddish-pink head and dripped off of its wings. Wet, reddish fluid. It stood atop a lifeless body. The coppery smell of blood was not as strong as it should have been considering the state of the body. There was a sweetness to the smell, a clearness to the fluid. It reminded her of the times she'd helped out with cattle birthing.

The bird cocked its head, the wideness of its black eyes making it look both sad and scared. A jagged scar marked one side of its face. The bird flapped its wings when Juana entered as if warning her away, its head bobbing forward. When she didn't move, it made a barking sound and coughed up a wad of semi-digested gray meat. And then another. A stream of urine ran down its leg. The wind created by the movement of its wings pushed the scent of ammonia and dead flesh her way, making her cough. She pulled her bandana over her mouth to block out the smell and ran at the bird waving her arms. The bird flapped its wings as it hopped past her, weaving like a borracho as it tried to fly. It went out the door and made a shaky flight to a nearby tree.

Juana coughed and turned away from the body and the smells the creature had left behind. The body belonged to a young woman. It looked like a discarded suit of torn skin and broken bones, blood and hair. It didn't look as though the vulture had eaten anything aside from her eyes.

"What do you think that was about?"

For the first time since she died, Analisa's mouth formed into a half-frown. The blood dripping from her ruined face fell in slow thick trails down to the ground forming a pool of black. No patterns this time. Only darkness.

Juana hadn't gone far when a woman on horseback flagged her down. "I'm looking for my friend," she said. "Have you seen anyone? She might have gone to . . . another friend's house."

Analisa stood next to the woman's horse, her blood dripping avian shapes in the dirt. "You can't tell her that she's dead."

"We don't know that it's her."

"What? What do you mean you don't know that it's her?" The woman looked warily at Juana.

"Do either of your friends live back that way?" The sigil on Juana's palm itched but she fought the urge to scratch it. Something was not right.

The woman nodded her head. "Yes. It's a long story, but the person who lived there is dead. They were close, though, like family. So she may have gone there. Did you see her?"

Juana turned her horse around. "Come with me."

A while later they stood under the shade of the trees, Eva's mouth set in a grim line. They had exchanged stories, Juana telling a bit of her background and how she came to the house, Eva relating what had happened in Soledad. Juana squeezed her hand open and shut, trying to stop the burning itch on her hand.

"I don't think your friend was killed by the same men you talked about," Juana said.

"Why do you think that? Who else would have killed her?"

Juana shook her head. "I don't know, but this doesn't feel right. It feels . . . different." She thought of the vulture that showed them the way. Was that the one that had been on top of the body? She didn't think so. That one felt . . . younger, somehow. Like it didn't know how to move right.

Eva shrugged. "It's all connected. Those *men.*" She

pronounced the word as though it sickened her. "It still comes back to them. Even if they didn't do this, they had a part in it."

"Isn't there a militia or a sheriff here?"

"Don Francisco kept order and acted as the sheriff, but after the war they sent a ranger and a group of men to disband the militia. They said they couldn't trust a Mexican to keep order." Eva spit. "That's when those pendejos moved in. They killed both Don Francisco and the Anglo who came in after him. You can't prove it, of course. Accidents they said, and no one much cares anyway. So, they say that Don Francisco shot himself accidentally while riding his horse. And Sheriff Brett just disappeared. They say he probably got bored and left, moved on somewhere else." She took a shaky breath. "It feels hopeless sometimes. Like the only thing we can do is leave, but if we leave they'll just chase us out of the next place or kill us. I was trying to make it work, but I wonder if it can."

"Let's go," Juana said.

Bloody footprints decorated the entry to Eva's Place. The door was open, but the wine-colored curtains remained over the large front window. Juana drew her knife and gestured for Eva to stay back. Eva ignored her and pulled a Colt from a pocket sewn into her voluminous skirt.

Blood marred the floor in a smeared trail leading from the bar to the piano. The tables had been pushed against one wall, some on their sides, chairs broken and thrown. Four women were laid out on the floor in front of the piano. One of them still had her hair tied up in rags. They had been trussed and gutted, stomachs gaping like large smiles from which long, coiled tongues protruded. Long cuts like symbols were carved into their thighs, arms, faces. Another woman lay on her side, a rib bone poking through her nightdress. A long cut ran across her forehead, and her nose had been sliced off. The skin on the back of her hands had been sliced off to expose the stark whiteness of her knuckles.

"This one fought back," Juana said.

"Mary Rose," Eva said. She looked at the others. "Isabel, Zulma, Diana."

Bloody tears dripped from Analisa's eye as she took in the carnage. They had been too late after all.

Eva's breathing grew louder. "No," she whispered when she saw Carolina in the corner. It looked like she had been dragged there. Her face was swollen with bruises, and her left arm and good chunk of her left side had been turned into a bloody pulp beside her body. Her right arm was up as if trying to deflect something, her palm sliced into stringy meat. "Oh, Carolina. She was protecting the children. They must have taken—"

Juana touched her arm and said, "First we need to see if anyone else is here. Is it possible that the children might be here somewhere?" She moved to look behind the bar and then headed for the stairs, stepping around spills of blood as she took them two at a time, Eva fast on her heels.

"Carolina's room was to the right, the second from the end."

A woman's body lay in the hall, face down. Her

back had been flayed open, a large hole like a budding rose in the center of the wound the bullet had made. Layers of skin had furled back like petals, displaying the muscular striations around the blackness where the bullet had entered, the skin lightly singed around it.

Eva whispered, "Margarita. If they came overnight, no one else would have been here. Hector would have gone home already."

They stepped around Margarita. Juana looked at Eva when she reached Carolina's room. "Let me look first."

"They're not here," Analisa said.

Juana looked and let out a sigh of relief. "They're not here," she said to Eva.

Eva crossed herself. They checked the rest of the rooms, looking under beds and in wardrobes, going back downstairs to check the storerooms and Eva's suite.

Too late. Juana traced the sigil on her hand and felt the weight of her knife in its hilt. Where could they be?

She walked back to the bar area where Eva had pulled up a bottle of whiskey and poured two glasses. They drank without pleasure, the warmth igniting a smoldering fire in Juana's belly.

She gestured toward a door. "Where does that go?"

"It's the back door . . . " She hurried to the door.

Juana touched Eva's arm, shaking her head.

A vulture circled overhead about 300 yards away. Juana started running, Eva right behind her. "Too late." Analisa's voice was a soft whisper in Juana's head.

Juana saw what happened just as if she had been there. They had been holding hands as they ran away. The girl lagged slightly behind the boy, and when the shot tore through her back she fell on her face and he lost his grip. The second blast caught him on the side of his neck as he turned to look for his sister. They lay in the golden grass, their blood darkening the soil. The boy's hand moved, and for moment Juana thought he might be alive. But it was just a shadow of the grass waving in the breeze.

"Pobrecitos, pobrecitos." Eva had bent over as though in pain. She kept repeating the word. Analisa stood next to Juana, silent for once, as she stared at Eva with pity, blood dripping onto the soft, rustling grasses.

The vulture overhead circled down slowly, eyeing Juana warily. It was the same vulture from the cabin, with the scarred face. It walked over and caressed the bodies with its beak, rubbing their small faces gently. A glimmer of moisture—a tear?—in its eye caught the sun. It began to feast, and a shadow fell over them as a second vulture circled for its descent.

The men were easy to find and easy to kill as they slept the easy sleep of murderers. The women shot them as they lay in their bunks, except for the two light sleepers who tried to escape. Their end was too quick in Juana's opinion, but it was more important to be done with it. Get rid of the pestilence quickly before it could spread.

"This must end," Eva said. "It's gone on for too long. Thank you."

Juana said nothing, and Analisa surprised her by also keeping quiet. The vulture woman in her dream had warned them that they needed to hurry, that it might be too late. She thought of the scarred vulture that had been in the house and in the field with the dead children. They had been too late. But she could at least avenge them, make sure that justice was served.

"And what about the next person you need to avenge? And the next after that?" Juana wanted to argue with Analisa but knew she was right. For now, though, they had to focus on finding Avery. He wasn't at the bunkhouse.

Eva took the lead, her black hair breaking free of its loose braid, streaming like her horse's mane as they galloped. Juana crouched in her saddle, looking around as they rode. They seemed to be heading for a small boxy house, its once yellow boards bleached by the sun. Its glass windows were shaded by what looked like horse blankets, the panes too dirty to reflect the sun. It looked deserted.

Eva dismounted and hobbled her horse to a sickly tree. Juana did the same. They'd walk the rest of the way.

The house was dark and musty, dust motes speckling the crack of sunlight from the open door. The wood floors were covered with dirty rag rugs and strewn clothing. The smell of Mae Beth's body hit them before they got to the door. She lay next to the bed, head resting on the wall, neck at an impossible angle.

Avery was standing outside of Eva's Place when they returned. He wore the same brown hat he had been wearing when Juana saw him in San Antonio, otherwise she may not have recognized him. His face had erupted in a raised red welts that had forced his eyes nearly shut. His sleeves were rolled up, a yellow-brown crusted piece of linen tied around his forearm. Deep purple veins formed paths around the deep red line stretching out from beneath the bandage to the heel of his hand. He coughed and spit a wad of green-yellow phlegm.

"You were in San Antone," he said. His voice was rough and nasal, and he sucked snot into the back of his throat so he could spit again. "You spyin' on me, Eva? I thought we were friends."

"We were never friends. Especially not after all you've done."

Juana stepped forward, wanting nothing more than to scream her rage at him. "If *I* had been her spy, I would have killed you then."

He hooted with laughter that turned to a cough that threatened to topple him over. "If anyone could do that, 'twouldn't be a thing like you." He gagged and finally spit out a wad of reddish-black phlegm the size of a silver dollar. A runner of snot ran from his nose and he wiped it off with the back of his hand, shaking it down into the dust. He winked. "I might be sick but I'm still quick on the draw."

The hate in Juana's eyes matched his own. She was more than ready. Her hand itched to grab her knife and throw it, watch it sink into his chest or his throat. Longed to jump on his back and stab and slash until nothing was left of him except strips of skin. But of course, he would want a gunfight. A man like him needed the extra power and distance of the gun. Her smile matched his own; she looked forward to killing him. Movement in her periphery made Juana glance to the left.

"So this is it?" Analisa asked? "Your big fight? Will this be the last one or the first of the rest of the last ones? How many more do you need? When will enough be enough?" The intact side of Analisa's mouth turned down. "This is what she was afraid of."

"Who?"

"Who what?" Avery responded.

Juana glared and clenched her mouth shut. When would she learn? She looked again and Analisa was gone, only her dark blood remaining. It formed a shape like wings.

Avery coughed again and shook his head like a dog. A mud-like smear remained under his nose. Juana's mouth curled in disgust. She could see his sweat beading and dripping down his face. She wanted to rush over and cut him, to savor the time she spent cutting him open.

"Let's do this," he said.

Eva's hand moved quicker than Juana would have thought it could as she pointed the Colt at him. Juana knocked Eva's hand down and drew her own gun. She didn't want him to die just yet. The first shot knocked Avery down, causing his shot to go through the front window of Eva' place. The second shot took a chunk of his right bicep. He fell to the ground with a gargling, angry moan.

"Don't kill him," Juana said. She had a plan.

They used Juana's reata to tie Avery's hands together in a complicated series of knots. His skin was clammy and seemed to crawl when they grabbed his wrists. The lumps on his face looked like they were ready to break open at the slightest pressure. She worked quickly, not wanting to touch him any more than she had to. He fainted after falling to the ground, breathing in loud snuffling inhalations. Juana imagined he would insist he had not fainted. But he wouldn't get the chance to say anything.

She sat high in the saddle, making sure the rope was secure around the saddle. People began to gather to see what was happening, but she had no time for an audience.

Eva nodded to Juana. She went to stand with the group.

Juana nodded back and dug her bootheels into the horse's side. She let out a whoop and yelled as she urged the horse faster. Her own yells drowned the noises Avery made as he was pulled behind. Juana was glad he had wakened long enough to feel the pain. She hoped it hurt every bit as much as the pain he'd inflicted on others. She rode to Jovita's house. *Rest well, vieja.* The horse turned in a half circle as they headed back toward Eva's Place. They picked up speed until Juana felt a jolt. The horse reared up and for a second Juana thought they would fall over, but it slammed its hooves down before breaking free of whatever had snagged their cargo.

They stopped in the field near Eva's. Juana cut the rope and swung down.

The red, dust-covered smear that was Avery lay on the brittle grass. She pushed it with her foot until the once-human lump turned over. His skin and clothes had been scraped to shreds. His left leg had been torn off at the calf. It must have gotten stuck in a rock when they were heading back. His face had been torn, his teeth and jaw shattered. The makeshift bandage on his arm had been torn away, exposing the pus and blood that had risen up beneath it.

Juana felt tired rather than exhilarated. She felt almost . . . sad. Not for Avery, but for everything that had happened before. She needed to sleep.

Analisa stood next to her with her usual half-grin in place. "You did good."

Eva walked over and kicked the bloody pile of rags and skin.

Two vultures soared high overhead.

"What will you do now?" Juana asked.

Eva looked overhead and gave a small smile. "I was thinking about pulling up stakes and moving on, but I might just stick around here for a while. There are things to clean up, people to take care of. Maybe tomorrow will be better. And you?"

Juana looked to Analisa who shrugged. "I don't know," she said. She wanted to move on. She was weary. Soledad was not the place for her. A long walk sounded good. Maybe she'd see if they needed a worker over at Las Nepantlas. She wanted to take time to look around her as she traveled. To look at the sky and the scenery as she considered her future. She and Analisa could talk the way they used to.

It was a long way back to Las Nepantlas, and she looked forward to seeing Yanina again.

ACKNOWLEDGEMENTS

The works of Jovita González and José Antonio López were instrumental in helping me learn about the true history of my native South Texas home. Any historical errors that I made were either done for creative reasons (such as taking some liberties with geography) or were my own mistake and not due to their research. I highly recommend their books if you are interested in learning about Tejano history and the ranchos established in what is now South Texas. The true stories are much more horrific than any fiction we can dream up.

Thank you to Jarod Barbee and Patrick C. Harrison III of Death's Head Press for giving me the opportunity to write a (counter)western of the splatter variety and for being patient as I worked my way through it.

Thank you to Brian Keene, Jackie Mitchell, Ryan Harding, John Urbancik, Kenzie Jennings, and V. Castro for various types of support during this process. Horror writers truly are the best people. A huge thank you to Kristin Wilson for her friendship and support.

Thank you also goes out to my family who surrounded me with stories of ghosts and witches and all kinds of grisly things growing up. I hope my own children enjoyed hearing those stories and embellished versions of them as much as I did.

Thank you to Eldritch, who contributed in ways they didn't realize. Special thank you to Hana Mitchell, brilliant writer and pre-reader extraordinaire.

I couldn't have done any of this without my partner and love, Joseph Mitchell, who always reminds me that there is time to read and write.

ABOUT THE AUTHOR

Regina Garza Mitchell grew up on the border of Texas and Mexico and now lives in the Midwest. She has twice been a writer-in-residence at Golden Apple Art Studio. She has published around 20 short stories in places like *In Laymon's Terms, Space and Time*, and *Campfire Macabre*. She is the co-editor (with David G. Barnett) of the *Big Book of Blasphemy*.

Without Excuse
The Compelling Evidence for Creation

Copyright January 2022
Julie Von Vett & Bruce A. Malone
Interior Layout and Design: Jamie Walton
Cover design: Jamie Walton

ISBN number: 978-1-939456-39-7
Library of Congress Control Number: 2021922765

Printed in China

All images used with permissions of:
Jamie Walton, Bruce Malone, NASA, iStock Photo

First Printing - January 2022

If this book has changed your outlook on life, strengthened your faith, or deepened your relationship with your Creator, please let us know. Low cost multiple copies are available using the order form at the back of the book or by visiting our ministry website (listed below).

May God bless you as you share the truth with others.

E-mail - truth@searchforthetruth.net
Web - www.searchforthetruth.net
Mail - 3255 Monroe Rd.; Midland, MI 48642
Phone – 989.837.5546

FOREWORD

We are rapidly returning to a time when majority opinion is accepted as synonymous with truth, and deviant perversions are justified by sinful desires. There is nothing new about this trend, because left unchanged, the human heart will always accept lies which leave God out rather than submit to His authority. Over 3,000 years ago, the previously unstoppable nation of Israel fell into the same situation, Judges ends with the sad commentary that, "In those days there was no King in Israel *(God was meant to be the King over every nation)*; every man did that which was right in his own eyes." – Judges 21:25

More than ever, it is critical to understand that God's Word forms the foundation for understanding morality, reality, history, and science. It is because we have a Creator that we can make sense of creation. The reality that creation has a Creator provides a reasonable explanation for the order we find in nature. Creation requires that there is an incredible creative intelligence, outside of the created universe, capable of bringing order from chaos. But it also means that morality is not fluid and changeable based on fallen human opinion and desire, but it is as absolute as the laws of science and does not change with time and culture. Through the Bible, humans have been given a true history of the universe through which we can properly interpret both history and scientific observations. Most importantly, it is by observing creation that we can know that God exists and know His characteristics.

God does not want us to **hope** He exists, **think** He exists, or **simply believe** He exists. Romans 1:18-24 is emphatically clear:

> [18] For the wrath of God is revealed from heaven against all ungodliness and unrighteousness of men, who hold the truth in unrighteousness; [19] Because that which may be known of God is [obvious]... [20] For the invisible things of him from the creation of the world are clearly seen, being understood by the things that are made, even his eternal power and Godhead; so that they are without excuse: [21] Because that, when they knew God, they glorified him not as God, neither were thankful; but became vain in their imaginations, and their foolish heart was darkened. [22] Professing themselves to be wise, they became fools...[24] wherefore God gave them up to [sinful desires]...